Richard was bringing the story to a close.

In the silence that followed, the twins sighed with sleepy satisfaction. They beamed at Richard, who smiled round at Kit, and the atmosphere in the bedroom seemed to catch and join, binding them close like a proper family. This is how it would be if we were married with children of our own. This thought rose unbidden to Kit's mind, and she was instantly appalled. But he belongs to Josie; he's not mine!

Dear Reader

We don't travel far this month, but there is compensation in welcoming back Elizabeth Harrison after a long absence—also Stella Whitelaw and Janet Ferguson. The warmth they generate between their characters is lovely, and I'm sure you'll find their romances fascinating. We also have Caroline Anderson back again after the mammoth work she put into her trilogy, moving out of the hospital setting to explore the problems encountered by a working mother in general practice. Lots of pleasurable reading!

The Editor

Janet Ferguson was born at Newmarket, Suffolk. She nursed as a VAD during the Second World War, then became a medical secretary, first working in hospital in London and the provinces, and now in Brighton near her home. She has had a number of novels published, but she finds Medical Romances the most satisfying and interesting to plot.

Recent titles by the same author:

THE DOCTORS AT SEFTONBRIDGE
ENCOUNTER WITH A SURGEON

LABOUR OF LOVE

BY

JANET FERGUSON

MILLS & BOON LIMITED
ETON HOUSE 18–24 PARADISE ROAD
RICHMOND SURREY TW9 1SR

First published in Great Britain 1993
by Mills & Boon Limited

This edition 1993

ISBN 0 263 78184 4

Set in 10 on 12 pt Linotron Times
03-9307-55757

Typeset in Great Britain by Centracet, Cambridge
Made and printed in Great Britain

CHAPTER ONE

The Parentcraft meeting was late breaking up; in fact it was nearly five-thirty when the chattering group of pregnant ladies filed out of the health centre doors.

Midwife Kit Greenham was sliding the chairs back against the walls when Richard Anstey—Dr Richard Anstey, to give him his proper title—strolled through from Reception. He had just come back from his calls.

Kit gave a nervous little start when she saw him standing there, straight and tall in the doorway, medical case in hand. Richard was engaged to her friend, Josie Brett, so she knew him personally, as well as through her work, and, minding what he thought, she wished he hadn't caught her on this warm April evening, feeling hot and bothered, with the ends of her belt hanging loose.

'How did it go?' he asked her, thrusting the glasses which he always wore for driving into the pocket of his suit. He was attractive with or without his glasses—a lean-cheeked, jet-haired man, with a wide mouth, discerning grey eyes, a quiet yet positive manner, and something about him—Kit sighed a little—that made a girl feel she'd move mountains if he asked her to, and climb up and down them as well.

'I think it went off all right,' she replied. 'Lots of questions were asked.'

'Shows you sparked their interest.' He watched her fastening her belt, affording him a view of the top of her head, of the straight centre parting in her corn-gold hair, which she wore in a jaw-length bob. She was taller than his fiancée, Josie, a stronger physical type. The two girls were the same age, he knew—twenty-six and a bit. They were friends of long-standing, even though their paths had diverged. He thought Kit looked a shade wearied this evening, but, as he knew well, taking a group through the finer points of relaxation was a tiring business, for seldom, if ever, did it benefit both sides. 'I think Jo said you're on call tonight.' He was moving back to the doors.

'I am, yes, but, with fingers crossed, all will be quiet,' she smiled.

'I hope so, for your sake.' He gave her a searching look, then turned and walked down the corridor leading to the main area, where four separate firms of general practitioners had their consulting rooms. He was the kind of man who arrived and departed with the minimum of fuss. There were often no greetings, or goodnights, or goodbyes; he simply came and went. A no-fuss type. Kit watched him punch his way through the first set of doors.

He was in partnership with his father, Dr Edward Anstey. Kit's mind was still on him as she made her way out to her car. They were a lovely family, really friendly, and soon Josie would be part of it—would become Mrs Anstey, instead of Mrs Brett.

Josie was a divorcée, with twin boys of seven years old. It was she who had persuaded Kit to apply for her present post. 'Give it a go, Kit; you're due for a change, and I'd love to have you here. If you get the job, and I don't see why you shouldn't, you could share my house. I'm dying for you to meet Richard; I know you'll like him. I just can't believe that he wants to marry me and take on the boys.'

All this had been just before Christmas, when Josie and Richard had been engaged only a matter of days. Josie had worked at the health centre then, as a part-time secretary, but had since resigned, for being engaged to Richard made it awkward, she said.

Kit landed the staff midwife's post, and had come to Melbridge-on-Thames during the third week in February, and was now, at the end of two months, a settled-down and well-liked member of the midwives' team.

As for her liking Richard, she had done so on sight. She respected him for his professionalism—he was an obstetrician, as well as a GP, and occasionally their paths crossed. As a woman she knew she was drawn to him, quite disturbingly attracted, but she tried not to let this worry her, for it had to be nothing more than the natural reaction of a girl to a man who had more than his share of good looks. Why, even Kit's mother, in late middle age, thought him a lovely man. . .'And he's so *unaware* of it, Kit, which isn't always the case!'

Mrs Elspeth Greenham, a widow, lived in the neighbouring town of Grantford. She was one of the reasons why Kit had returned to her roots, leaving the Midlands, where she had done her training and practised afterwards. Kit was a qualified nurse as well as a midwife. 'My daughter is thorough,' Mrs Greenham liked to boast. 'She never does things by halves.'

Even though they were friends, Kit had been surprised at Josie offering her living space. Being newly engaged, and with Richard coming round, surely she wouldn't want anyone else at the Russell Road house—but it seemed that Josie did. 'I'll make the largest bedroom into a bed-sit for you,' she had enthused over the phone. 'That way we can both have privacy whenever we want. Most of the time, anyway, Richard and I will be going out, and think how useful you'll be as a living-in baby-sitter!' Kit had laughed, for this was typical Josie, and the arrangement, up until now, had worked well. . .was *still* working well. . . She made the firm correction, underlining it in her mind, as she turned down Russell Road.

The house which had been Josie's marital home sprang into view once she had passed the villa-type ones at the top of the road. It was white-stuccoed and double-fronted, with a green front door. One of the downstairs windows was open, and even before she halted the car in the drive she could hear the telephone ringing. It might not be for her, of course, but she had a feeling it was. Scrambling out of the car and into the house, she grabbed the receiver seconds before Josie had got within feet of it.

She was right too: it was for her—the husband of one of her expectant mothers. His voice came jerkily into her ear. 'It's Guy Jevons, Nurse. I'm worried about Claire. She's in a lot of pain—has been since four o'clock. She says it isn't the baby, but it might be, mightn't it? Can you possibly come?'

'How often are the pains coming?' Kit asked, bringing Claire Jevons to mind. She was thirty-seven weeks on in her pregnancy and booked for a domino delivery. Kit had promised her that she would try to be on hand when labour began, and had given her husband her bleep and home number, with the hospital base one as well.

'She's in pain all the time—it doesn't go—and she's

got a headache too. She feels sick and awful!' Guy Jevons was saying, and Kit delayed no more.

'Quite right to ring,' she said. 'I'll be with you in a few minutes. It may be just a tummy upset, but I'll come along to make sure.' She was checking her obstetric bag when Josie came out of the kitchen. Behind her, sitting up at the long pine table, the two little boys, Daniel and Harry, were having their supper-tea. 'I've got to go out, Jo. It's one of my dominoes.' Kit turned to the door, ignoring the shouts of the twins, who liked to have her around at their bath-time, for she always made it fun.

'Oh, well, rather you than me!' Josie waved her off, standing at the top of the steps, her flaxen hair floating round the shoulders of her pale blue leisure suit.

Guy Jevons wasn't the sort to panic, but his long, bony face was the colour of putty when he answered the door to Kit's ring. His wife was upstairs, half sitting, half lying on the bed. 'Oh, I'm glad to see you. . . I'm glad you're here!' she gasped, and clutched Kit's wrist. Her face was swollen; so were her hands. Kit noticed this at once.

'Where exactly is the pain, Claire?' She sat on the side of the bed.

'Here, high up.' Caire indicated her epigastric region.

So not contractions. Alarm bells began to ring in Kit's head. 'And where's your headache. . .back or front?'

'Front, right over my eyes, and *in* them too, like a migraine, making me feel sick!' She was still wearing slippers and her ankles were swollen right over the tops. Kit's alarm mounted as she took her sphygmomanometer from her case.

'We'll see what your blood-pressure reading is; that may explain a lot,' she said more cheerfully than she felt, wrapping the tourniquet cuff round Claire's upper arm, trying not to show her face. Her worst fears were confirmed, however. Claire's blood-pressure was dangerously high—160 over 110. She could easily have a fit. All her symptoms were clearly indicative of severe pre-eclampsia. She would have to be transferrred to hospital with the utmost urgency.

Still maintaining a calm front, Kit told the young couple that as Claire's blood-pressure had gone very high she would be better in hospital, where she would be given treatment to bring it down, and be cared for generally. There was no need to alarm them, yet there was every need to stress the importance of hospital treatment, especially as Guy was looking sceptical, even stubborn. 'It's not what we planned,' he said.

'I know, but this is unexpected.' Kit was moving out of the room.

'Will the baby be all right?' Claire cried.

'If we act quickly, I'm sure it will.' And, please God, let me be speaking the truth. . . Kit was at the head of the stairs. 'I'll ring for an ambulance, then come back and talk to you both. Perhaps you could draw the curtains, Guy—the light is right in Claire's eyes—and pack a bag for her, just a nightdress and toilet things.' She was downstairs at last, lifting the phone, dialling the County Hospital. The obstetric flying squad came out from there, and wouldn't take long to arrive. She gave rapid details, then rang Richard, for he was Claire Jevons's GP. Thursday wasn't his night for surgery and, with luck, he'd be at home. He lived very near, only two roads away; he'd need to know what was going on.

He must, Kit thought, have been near the phone, for he answered it after two rings. 'Richard Anstey speaking.' His deep-toned voice skimmed the top off her fears.

'Richard, it's Kit Greenham. I'm at eleven Marks Road. Your patient, Mrs Jevons, is showing all the signs of severe pre-eclampsia. I've sent for the squad, but I thought that perhaps—'

'Be with you in five minutes,' was his quick reply, then she heard his phone go down.

Back upstairs she talked to Claire in as relaxed a manner as possible, getting her to lie back on the bed with a pillow under her knees, persuading her husband, who had packed her bag, to take it downstairs and get the front door open ready for the flying squad.

Richard was the first to arrive, swiftly injecting Claire with an anti-hypertensive drug to start off the process of getting her rising blood-pressure down. During the few minutes' interval before the ambulance came, he chatted to her quietly, making her feel that being rushed off to hospital was no big deal. Kit, meantime, was jotting down details of her blood-pressure, temperature and pulse, the size of her uterus, the baby's heart-rate and exactly how it was lying, for these details—base-line though they were—would be helpful to the hospital staff.

They heard the ambulance sirening its way through the traffic lights in the High Street, but it was sneakily quiet as it drew up outside the house, and an obstetrician of registrar status, followed by a young midwife, followed by two ambulancemen, thudded up the stairs.

Claire was reassured, further sedated, then conveyed to a stretcher of the chair variety, and carried out to the waiting ambulance. It drew away, gathered speed, and was soon lost to sight, followed by a tense-faced Guy Jevons in his landscape-gardening van.

'So long as she doesn't start to fit, they're likely to do a Caesarean section in a matter of hours, to save the child,' Richard observed.

'I suppose so, yes.' Kit glanced back to make sure that the house door was closed.

'Good thing Jevons sought help quickly.'

Kit nodded in agreement, feeling for her keys. Then, as she and Richard stood by their cars, neither making a move to get in, they heard the wail of the ambulance again, and imagined its diving rush through the town and up the hill, into the hospital yard.

'She's had such a normal, uneventful pregnancy up until now,' said Kit. 'It was so unexpected; I felt really shocked when I saw her tonight.'

'I know what you mean, but, as we *both* know, pre-eclamptic toxaemia of pregnancy can be an unheralded condition. Its cause is still something of a mystery to the medical scientists.'

From the town centre St Martin's Church began to chime the hour. Six-thirty; was that all it was? Kit had the feeling that hours had passed since Josie had waved her off from the steps. 'I suppose we'd better be going.' She bent to unlock her car.

'Yes, time's getting on,' he agreed, watching her place her 'little black bag' on the passenger seat and slide behind the wheel. 'Could I ask a favour?' His enquiry came quickly, almost as an afterthought.

'Why, yes, of course. . .ask away!' Anything, she thought. Anything, just anything—you name it; it shall be done. Perhaps he was going to ask her to move those mountains after all. But no, it was something far easier and more commonplace.

'Could you,' he went on 'follow me along to my house? I've got some eggs for Jo, and I'd like her to have them. I can't bring them round myself, not tonight, as I've got my parents coming to supper. They're the real McCoy—free-range—but I'll never get through a dozen. They were given me by a patient who keeps hens on his back lawn!'

'Good for him!' Kit swallowed against a flutter of disappointment. For Jo—well, naturally. What else had she expected?

'Lead on, I'll follow,' she said, stretching her face in a grin. So they both did a U-turn in the road, Kit following his blue Peugeot up the road, into the High Street, past the war memorial and the palatial façade of the Bridge Hotel, into Palmerstone Drive.

She had seen Richard's house in passing several times, and, although she had peered out at it, she had never actually stopped and had a good look at it, as she was able to do now. It was a large-ish house, five-bedroomed; Josie had told her that. It had a homely look about it, with its mellowed red-brick walls, its lattice windows and lichened roof, and a way of resting comfortably on the river-green lawns that panned away from its sides.

The house had been bequeathed to Richard by his maternal grandmother. It was here that Josie and the twins would be living after the wedding. It would be a perfect home for them; they would all be secure. Josie deserved it; she deserved happiness, someone to rely on. Richard would never let her down; he was as steady as a rock, yet fun to be with, and he loved the twins, as they did him.

Kit watched him slam his way out of the Peugeot and go in to get the eggs. Even from the back he looked attractive—dark head held very high, his suit just a little loose, perhaps, long legs moving smoothly and effortlessly, in line with the rest of him.

He had been living at the house since Easter, employing a daily housekeeper, the widow of one of his patients who had recently died. Kit wondered if the housekeeper did the garden as well, for surely Richard didn't have time to keep it as it was now? It was awash with bulbs, little seas of narcissi and streams of daffodils. She could smell hyacinths, glimpse spikes of forsythia breaking yellow at the side of the house. There was a gazebo with a coned top; the twins would love that. She was still blatantly staring when Richard came out with the eggs.

'Like it?' He sounded amused.

'I was having a good look,' Kit admitted, 'and yes, I do like it, very much indeed. In this light, with the sun going down, it's like a picture out of a book.'

'*Homes and Gardens*?' he was teasing, and she flicked a glance at him.

'No, a children's book more; there's magic there.'

'Yes, I know,' he responded at once. 'I've felt that at times. So did my grandmother; she and I were close.' He handed her the eggs, still watching her as she laid the box on the seat, noticing how the same sun that was mantling his garden had turned her hair to a singing yellow stranded with red-gold. 'Come in and look round, if you'd like to.' He made to open her door.

'Oh, no, I don't think so.' Her refusal came quickly

and she saw the surprise in his eyes. 'I'm on call,' she explained, knowing that five minutes wouldn't make very much difference, 'and you're expecting your parents.' Even as she spoke, the big grey Volvo belonging to the senior doctor and his wife hove into sight, rounding the corner at the top of the road. Her relief showed. 'Here they are now; I'll move off and let them turn in.' Switching on the engine and letting off the handbrake, she drew away from the kerb, raising a hand to Dr Edward and his wife as the two cars met and passed.

But why, she wondered, as she turned the corner, had she refused Richard's invitation? What could be more innocuous than being shown over a house and garden? She knew the answer to that, of course; she didn't really have to wonder. The answer, or reason, was that she didn't want by so much as a breath to like him more, to be attracted to him more than she already was. The demarcation line between what she felt now and what she *could* feel was too close for comfort. . . dangerously close. Richard was Josie's fiancé, and to fall in love with him would be asking for unhappiness, courting frustration. Things might become so impossible that she would have to leave her job.

Josie was surprised to see her back so soon, and delighted with the eggs. 'Good, we can have omelettes for supper, unless you get called out again.'

'Somehow or other, I don't think I will be.' Kit reached for a basin and whisk.

'Did Richard ask you in?' Josie glanced at her. 'Did you see over the house? What did you think of it—old-fashioned, isn't it? I couldn't live in it like that. Richard has promised me a complete refurbishment—that's really why we aren't getting married until September. It's an old lady's house.'

'I didn't see inside; I only stopped at the gate. Richard was expecting his parents.' Kit broke the first egg clumsily, and got shell mixed up with the yolk.

'Yes, I know; that's why he couldn't come round tonight. He wanted me to make up the four, but I knew you were on call, and I don't like leaving the twins with just anyone. Richard's a great one for family obligations.'

'That's no bad thing.'

'No, of course it isn't, and I'm just the same, up to a point. Talking of families——' Josie slipped off the stool and went to the dresser drawer '—Mum rang up this morning. She and Dad are driving up to town next Tuesday, just for the day. They want me to meet them, and I'd like to; it's ages since I saw them. So I thought I'd go up early, after I've dropped the kids off at school. Mrs Miller will collect them in the afternoon, when she fetches her own. She'll feed them and keep them at her place till you finish your shift. You can pick them up from there, can't you?' She was talking very fast, banging the dresser drawer shut, turning round with the cloth. 'I shall be home at seven, long before Richard turns up, but if you could give them their bath and settle them down it would help no end.'

'As I'm not going out that evening, fine,' Kit said after a pause, then added quickly, 'yes, of course I'll do it,' and smiled at her friend. The truth was she adored the twins, and loved having charge of them, but occasionally, just very occasionally, Josie needed to be reminded that Kit had a social life of her own.

The Telfords, Josie's parents, ran a group of hotels

on the south coast. Usually, when they came to London to visit their head office, they made the extra journey to Melbridge to see their small grandsons. This time, it seemed, it wasn't going to be possible. 'They can't manage it,' Josie said, turning her back on Kit to spread the cloth over the table, 'but they can see them in the holidays, and I may even decide to take them down to Eastbourne at half-term.'

After their meal of omelettes and crispy French bread, the two young women settled down to watch a film on TV. Kit's thoughts kept straying to Claire Jevons. What was happening to her? It would be pointless to ring the hospital too soon. She would wait until after ten, then speak to the night sister on duty, whom she knew quite well. As things turned out, however, she didn't need to do so, for at a little after ten o'clock the telephone rang just as she was standing by it ready to dial. She lifted the receiver. 'Kit Greenham here.'

'My goodness, that was quick!' It was Richard.

'I was standing by the phone.'

'The news of Claire Jevons is good,' he hurried to reassure her, hearing the anxiety in her voice.

'Oh, I'm *glad*! I've been wondering about her all evening.' Kit stretched an arm backwards to close the sitting-room door against the blare of the ten o'clock news.

'I've just this moment,' Richard was saying, 'been on to the hospital and spoken to Clive Rossiter, who did a Caesar an hour ago, the result being a healthy baby girl with an Apgar score of seven, and a yell loud enough to be heard in the street outside! Guy Jevons, the first to hold his daughter, is apparently over the moon.'

'And his wife. . .what about. . .how is Claire?' Kit enquired.

'Fine. . .condition stable, although she'll feel grim for a day or two. She'll need careful nursing and close supervision, but all the signs are good.'

'I'll probably delay visiting until after the weekend,' Kit started to say, then broke off, for Josie had appeared.

'If that's Richard, after you,' she was mouthing, so, thanking him for letting her know, Kit handed over the receiver, and went tactfully up to her room.

By Tuesday Claire Jevons was fully ambulant, moving about the post-natal ward, getting told off by the sister for not straightening up. 'It's all very well for her; she's not the one with the stitches!' Claire said ruefully, when Kit slipped in to see her at lunchtime. 'Still, I suppose she's right. I don't want to look like a geriatric too soon!'

'I hear you're breast-feeding very successfully. We're all pleased with you, Claire.' Kit felt that praise was due, for the girl had been through a bad time.

'It's all right in here, but I'll be glad to get home.' Claire's eyes strayed to the cot at the side of her bed, where baby Angela was screwing up her face. 'She's not bad, is she?'

'She's gorgeous. Guy must be proud of you both.'

Claire laughed carefully, mindful of her wound. 'Guy's walking around with his feet six inches above the ground at the moment. My mother is at home looking after him, so I don't have to worry.'

'That's half the battle, isn't it?' Kit was getting up to go. She had a full afternoon's list and wanted to finish on time. This was the day she was due to bath the twins and get them to bed.

They were ready and waiting for her when she got to the Millers' house in Crantock Road, just before half-past five.

'Johnnie Miller eats with his mouth open,' Daniel said in the car.

'But we had a nice tea—fish fingers and beans,' Harry reminded him. 'I'm glad we're going home now. I like our house better, and Mummy said she'd leave us some raspberry ripple in the fridge.'

'You'd better not have too much of that. . .after fish fingers and beans.' Kit flinched at the thought, as she nudged the car into the traffic stream. Once home, she changed into jeans and sweater, and played rounders with the boys in the back garden, after scaling down their portions of ice-cream. At six-thirty she ran their bath and got them both into it. They could bath themselves, with supervision, but drying was more difficult. She was helping them with this, rubbing their backs with big, soft towels, when the doorbell rang. 'Who's that, I wonder?' She got up from her knees.

'It can't be Mummy; she's got her own key,' Daniel was quick to point out.

'And she won't be home yet. . .not until seven. I expect it's Richard!' Harry, busy with his pyjama jacket, could have had no idea of the effect his words had on Kit who, dropping Daniel's towel, sped almost unwillingly down the stairs, palming her hair down flat. Part of her hoped that it wasn't Richard, yet her immediate reaction when she got the door open and saw him there on the step was one of sharp pleasure which she was powerless to hide.

'Josie's not back yet, but come in.' She closed the door behind him. 'I've just got the boys out of the bath, so I'd better get back to them. The evening paper is in the sitting-room, if you'd like to look at it. I shan't be long; it's just a matter of. . .' She broke off as he shook his head.

'I came early on purpose, with the idea of helping.' He smiled down at her, his face in shadow. Josie's hall was the darkest part of the house. 'I know,' he went on, 'what a handful those two lads can be.'

'Richard! Richard! We thought it was you!' The two young lads, wildly excited, appeared on the landing, jumping up and down. 'Are you going to tell us a story? Will you tell us a story in bed? We want to know more about Willie and Julian, who turned into garden gnomes!' The request came from Daniel, who was halfway down the stairs, pyjama trousers at half-mast. Kit hauled them up for him.

'Don't let them browbeat you, Richard,' she said. 'They can read for themselves, you know.'

'It's all right, I don't mind.' He watched her smoothing Daniel's hair out of his eyes, saw the quick kiss she gave him, before sending him back up the stairs. 'The more time I can spend with them, the easier it will be when the big transition takes place and I assume my father role.'

'True enough,' Kit laughed as they climbed the stairs together. She turned to the bathroom. 'I'll leave you to it, while I mop up this overspill.'

He's practically their father now, she thought, hanging wet towels up and opening the bathroom window to let out some of the fog. They rely on him already. . . look to him to do parent-orientated things, like telling them stories in bed. All this she could see on their faces when she went through into the bedroom, her own face pink with exertion, the front of her jeans dark-splashed.

Richard was sitting on a low stool between the two single beds. He was well into the story, which he was telling out of his head. 'But when summer was done, and autumn came, and the garden was cold and wet, they longed to be little boys again, and live in a proper house. . .' His voice was expressive; so were the illustratory gestures he made. Kit was careful not to interrupt, lowering herself into a chair by the window, watching the little tableau as though it was being played out on a stage. There were the children upright in bed and the dark-haired man on the stool, intent on involving them in the story, taking them step by step into the land of make-believe, where all things were possible.

A feeling of sadness and gladness mixed washed over Kit in waves—a shivery feeling that had nothing to do with being cold or afraid. What *was* it about Richard Anstey that made her react like this? From where she was sitting she could only see his back and part of his face—the angle of his jaw, the shape of his head, his hands making swooping movements to describe the way the witch rode her broomstick in and out of the clouds. He was bringing the story to a close now, his voice was changing again. . .'And the witch was pleased with the way they'd behaved, so she agreed to change them back into their real selves again, and by Guy Fawkes' night they were William and Julian Brookes once more, having a bonfire party, with jacket potatoes, and sausages, and lots of fireworks.'

In the silence that followed the twins sighed with sleepy satisfaction. They beamed at Richard, who smiled round at Kit, and the atmosphere in the room seemed to catch and join, and become a charmed circle, drawing them together, binding them close like a proper family, mother, father and sons. This is how it would be if we were married with children of our own. This thought rose unbidden to Kit's mind, and she was instantly appalled. But he belongs to Josie; he's not mine! What on earth am I thinking about?

'We liked the story, thank you,' said Harry. He was the first to speak, then came the sound of a car in the drive, the bite of tyres on gravel.

'That's Mummy! Mummy's home!' Daniel shouted joyfully.

'I expect it is.' Kit was nearest the window. She got up and looked out, just in time to see Josie paying off her taxi. 'Yes, it *is* Mummy,' she said shakily. She heard Richard get to his feet, then turned round to see the twins throwing back their duvets, getting out of their beds, and streaking to the door and down the stairs to greet their mother.

Richard laughed and threw up his hands. 'That's kids for you!' he said.

'But they loved your story; so did I.' Kit swallowed against a throat that seemed to have closed, and she couldn't meet Richard's eye.

'It's great to have children to entertain.' He was setting the stool back against the dressing-table, and taking his time about it.

'I know what you mean,' Kit said quietly, then Josie was in the room, elegant in her black suit with its straight, above-the-knees skirt, her pale hair shawling her shoulders, face raised for Richard's kiss.

'You're angels, both of you. . .doing my chores!' Her

smile included Kit. 'Now, you two, settle down!' She shooed the twins into their beds, informing Richard, in answer to his query, that yes, her parents were fine. 'They sent their love, were sorry not to see you.' She was talking over her shoulder, drawing the curtains over the window, pulling off the jacket of her suit. 'Kit will be here all the time, darlings.' She kissed her sons goodnight. 'Behave yourselves, now; see you in the morning.'

'In the morning, Mummy.' Half-asleep, they watched the three grown-ups filing from their room.

Josie pressed Kit to join her and Richard for a drink downstairs. 'We're not going out for half an hour, so there's plenty of time. I could do with a snifter; I'm just about bushed, and crippled as well.' She kicked off her high-heeled courts before going down the stairs. Kit set them inside Josie's bedroom as she passed it, but turned down the invitation.

'Thanks all the same, Jo, but no. There's a programme on the radio I want to hear, and it's just about to start. Have a good evening; enjoy the play.' She knew they were going off to the Theatre Royal in Grantford to see *The Barraclough Destiny*.

Once in her room she switched on the radio, but the concert she'd been looking forward to fell on deaf ears, for she couldn't concentrate. All her thought processes were focused on Richard, and wouldn't be dislodged. Presently the click of the front door closing told her that he and Josie were leaving the house and, going to the window, she waved, as she always did, giving a thumbs-up sign to show that all was well.

My middle name ought to be Cinderella, she thought ruefully, turning down the radio in case it disturbed the twins. But the situation during the following two weeks changed radically, in that she could no longer make a joke about it all. It was as though her feelings had crystallised, had become clear to her, and, looking back, she realised that the story-telling evening with Richard had been a veritable watershed. She was in love with him; she knew that. There was no might, or maybe. Now, when she saw him coming to the house, saw him and Josie setting off, laughing and talking together, the feeling of desolation which had once been transient, and which could have been simple envy, was changed to a deep-seated pain which stayed with her afterwards, refusing to be dislodged.

Something would have to be done; she knew that. She would have to leave Josie's house. She would have to go home to Grantford to live; she would have to get out of range. She didn't want to, and yet she must. . . She wavered for two more weeks, then in mid-May she told herself that enough was enough. Waking in the small hours one morning, staring at the light seeping under bedroom curtains, she began to rehearse what she was going to say to Josie, who must never know the truth.

CHAPTER TWO

JOSIE was giving the twins their breakfast when Kit left the house that morning. 'See you tonight!' they called out through mouthfuls of buttered toast.

'See you!' She flapped a hand and made for the door, her stomach lurching at the thought of what tonight would mean—tackling Josie, and she certainly wasn't looking forward to that. If I didn't mind about her, didn't mind upsetting her, it would be simple, she thought, crossing the drive to the garage and backing out the car. And not being able to tell her the true reason why she was leaving, meant a certain amount of judicious lying which had got to sound plausible.

The church clock was striking eight as she drove through the town. Someone waved to her—Enid Lawton with her baby. She was most likely, Kit knew, taking him to the minder, for she had a part-time job. Having a job was important to some young mothers, quite apart from the money side. Others preferred not to miss a single day of their child's development. Kit had an open mind and could understand both points of view.

Regarding her own job, she was going to pull out all the stops to keep it. She felt she would be able to do so, because meeting Richard professionally was a far cry from seeing him off-duty with Josie. To a certain extent, he seemed a different man when he was working. . .still attractive, very much so. . .but she could view him at those times as a doctor, and forget the rest. . .or so she told herself. Anyway, she reasoned, steering past a loaded builder's lorry, unless there are pregnancy complications, which don't occur all that often, I'm not working cheek-by-jowl with him, apart from in the clinics, and occasionally in his surgery when I need prescriptions signed. It will be all right. Take heart, Kit Greenham. You can do it if you try.

Even so, when she saw Richard locking his car on the health centre forecourt a few minutes later, she had to start acting with speed. He spotted her and came striding over, dark against the sun, his jacket and tie flying back in the wind. In spite of the sun it was chilly, and Kit felt he should wrap up more. She was glad of the warmth of the sweater she'd pulled on over her uniform dress.

'I've not seen you to talk to lately.' He waited for her to get out.

'Oh, it's just that our paths haven't crossed,' she said airily. 'You know how it is.'

He didn't, but said nothing more as she slammed her car door shut, looking at him only briefly, as though, even now, she wasn't especially pleased to see him standing there. 'I put a copy referral letter in your tray last night,' he informed her as they started to walk towards the health centre doors. 'It's to the hospital, *re* a Mrs James of Upper Clements Street. She's due to give birth at Christmas, possibly the week before. Can you fit in a first visit this afternoon, do you think? I told her a midwife would be calling on her around four or five o'clock.'

Kit relaxed. This was better; this was business only.

She even smiled at him. 'Yes, of course, no problem,' she said. 'I'll pick up the letter now.'

'Many thanks.' They parted quickly, once they got inside. His surgery began at half-past eight; so did her shift. She ought to be on the road right now. Hurrying to the office, she found the letter in the midwives' tray, then, saying goodbye to the three secretaries, who already looked harassed, she returned to her waiting car.

She liked to visit new mothers and their babies in the mornings, if possible, and mothers-to-be in the afternoons. Her first visit this morning was to a Mrs Libbots, who lived out at Crayton, a small village covered by two different doctors' surgeries.

Discounting the cold wind, it was a perfect May day, and in spite of everything Kit's spirits rose as she looked about her—at the blue-washed sky, at the poplars in the distance, at the flowering trees in cottage gardens, at the river glimpsed in flashes as it raced towards the weir.

Jill Libbots lived in Riverside Lane in an old-type bungalow which was built on stilts, and had steps all round, making it look like a dais. Leaving the car, climbing the steps, Kit was just about to knock when Jill came to the door with five-day-old Gemma in her arms. 'I've only just got her off,' she said, a shade complainingly.

'In that case, we won't wake her yet but see to you first.' Kit followed her into the bedroom, looking out of the window while she laid the baby back in her carry-cot. A barge loaded with grit from the quarry was chugging upriver, and two swans rocked in its wake; further along the bank an angler was reeling in his line.

'Lovely to live right on the river,' Kit remarked, as Jill straightened up.

'This time of the year, yes, but it can be dreary in the winter. It would be different if Mark was here all the time.' Jill began to unbutton her dress.

'But you've got near neighbours.' All along the bank were similar bungalows. Kit could see washing hanging out.

'Most of them are only here in the summer; their bungalows are second homes. Still, I've got the baby now, and Mark should be on leave round about the end of July, or even before that.' Jill's husband was in the Royal Navy, and although he'd been home for the birth he'd had to return to his ship very soon afterwards. This, Kit felt, was tough on Jill, although she knew she had a sister at Grantford, who came over whenever she could.

An episiotomy had been performed when Gemma was born. Kit had a look at Jill's stitches, telling her they were fine. 'But don't be afraid to massage yourself gently when you wash, and keep up your pelvic exercises to get the blood going round. All that will assist healing, make you look as good down in that region as you did before the birth. How are you getting on feeding Gemma?' she enquired, as Jill got dressed.

'I think all right.' Jill hesitated. 'She certainly likes my milk, but just look at the size of my breasts! Whatever is Mark going to say? I've *never* been this size!'

'They won't stay like that.' Kit didn't laugh, for she knew she wasn't meant to. 'You'll go back to your pre-pregnancy size in around four weeks' time. You'll still be able to keep feeding Gemma, though. . .long after that. Actually, Jill—' she popped a thermometer under the young mother's tongue '—you're doing amazingly well; you've nothing to worry about.'

It was the baby's turn next. She was undressed and weighed, her temperature taken in one tiny armpit, her eyes gently bathed. She had sticky eyes, which worried Jill, but again Kit reassured her. 'As the hospital told you, it's not uncommon for babies to have sticky eyes. It's caused by the tear ducts not being fully open. Keep bathing them twice a day like this; I'll leave you some saline. By the time the health visitor takes over from me, Gemma should be starry-eyed.'

'Will it be you tomorrow?' Jill took the baby, handling her a shade awkwardly, for, like all new roles, the natural one of motherhood still needed to be learned.

'No, Tessa will be coming tomorrow, but it'll be me again on Thursday.'

'Great to have all this supervision.'

'That's the name of the game!' Kit smiled, writing up her notes and repacking her bag.

She had another mother to visit in Crayton—an unmarried girl. She lived with her parents near the donkey sanctuary in a road called Gravelpit Lane. Kit could see the donkeys in their paddock as she passed, see the two elderly sisters who ran the place pitchforking hay about.

Rose Garner was eighteen and her boyfriend had been killed six months ago, one foggy morning, in an accident on the motorway. This Kit had learned from Rose's mother, who was anxious to establish that the two *had* intended to marry before the baby was born. Baby Tom was just two weeks old now. He'd been born at the County Hospital in eight hours flat with the minimum of fuss. 'He just shot out,' Rose was fond of telling everyone. She was dark-haired and dimpled, plump and placid, and plainly adored her son. Seeing her this morning showing him the garden, and pointing out the birds, Kit felt that she had probably loved his father very much indeed.

When Rose saw her and came walking towards her, smiling and saying, 'Mum's out,' Kit felt relieved, although she tried her best not to show it too much. Mrs Garner was a perfectionist, and examining baby Tom and Rose with her proffering advice and getting in the way was off-putting to say the very least. She was convinced that Kit was doing everything wrong, and that only she—a mother herself—knew what was best for her daughter and Tom. Her presence never bothered Rose, but then she, Kit thought, is just about the most laid-back female I've ever come across.

Taking Tom out of his sling, she weighed him and checked him over. He was blue-eyed with a shock of black hair, and looked the picture of health. He even had dimples like his mother, who was feeding him on demand. 'Saves so much aggro,' she told Kit, 'and it suits him too. He sleeps for seven hours every night, and so does his mum!' She lifted the baby high in the air as Kit handed him over, then laid him gently in the Moses basket, which an assiduous Mrs Garner had brought down from the attic prior to his birth.

After Rose had been examined, she offered Kit coffee, which the latter had to refuse, as she was running late and had three more visits to make before lunch. Rose went to the gate with her, eating a chocolate bar, seeming to want to talk. 'I'd like to get away from here, away from home,' she said. 'Perhaps I could get an au pair's job abroad, taking Tom with me, of course. I really do feel I need a change.' Looking swiftly at her, Kit surprised a look of sadness on the girl's plump face.

'It's early days yet, Rose; don't rush things,' she said, carefully choosing her words. 'You really need to be at home; you need your own family right now. Apart from anything else, it's only a fortnight since Tom was born. It's too soon to be making plans for moving away.' She very nearly added, 'And you're very young,' but bit that back in time, for Rose had probably heard it non-stop over the past few months.

'I shall go, though, before very long,' Rose said stubbornly, throwing the wrapper of her chocolate bar over the neighbour's hedge.

Kit felt every one of her twenty-six years as she turned the car and drove back to Melbridge with her mind still on Rose. By the time Rose was twenty-six her son would be eight years old, a whole year older than Daniel and Harry were now. This swung her thoughts to Josie and to moving out of the house. How would Josie react? Not well—Kit knew that— which was why she was feeling so much apprehension about tackling her friend. Being her friend, her oldest friend, didn't blind Kit to her faults. Josie's parents had always indulged her, and she liked her own way more than most. When she didn't get it, or when things went wrong, she could be a pain. The thing was that she liked Kit living with her, and had said so time and again. There was bound to be a fuss, bound to be a row, when the crunch came tonight.

And as for her mother. . . Kit braked at the lights;

she would need a little notice. It would hardly be fair to just walk in on her and say, 'Here I am.'

Mrs Greenham had recently taken in a lodger, the son of a friend of hers. Kit had met Andrew Gordon and liked him; she had been out with him once or twice. He had come to the south from his native Edinburgh to take up a teaching post at the Dartings, a prestigious boys' school in the centre of Melbridge. Ford House—Kit's home—was commodious and four-bedroomed, so there would be plenty of room for them all. Even so, she reasoned fairly, her mother would need to be warned. She had been very understanding when Kit had got her post in the Thames area and had told her that she intended sharing Josie's house. 'You see, it's so convenient, Mother, being near the midwives' base, and the health centre, and town centre. . . You *do* see what I mean?'

'I'm not in my dotage yet, darling.' Mrs Greenham had smiled. 'I don't need looking after, and *you* need young company. So go ahead and make your plans. It's enough for me that you'll be within easy reach now, and not miles away up north.'

Elspeth Greenham had been forty when Kit was born, so it was all the more surprising that she had never clung to nor made demands on her one and only child. Her husband had died two years ago, and very soon afterwards she had put herself up for voluntary work at the County Hospital. Since Christmas she had been the library lady, pushing a trolley of books round the surgical and medical wards three afternoons a week.

It was to the hospital that Kit drove when she had finished her morning visits. As this was the official midwives' base, she was allowed to use the canteen up on the fifth floor, which, as well as being central, had built-in advantages in that she could meet and chat to the hospital midwives over her bangers and mash. She could also, if time allowed, slip along to Maternity and have a word with one or two of her new-delivered mums. They were usually thrilled to show off their babies, and to describe their labour in graphic detail, finishing up with, 'It wasn't nearly as bad as I'd feared,' or, 'Never again; I've told my husband if he wants another he can jolly well have it himself.' So, yes, the comments were various, although it was truly amazing how the mothers who'd vowed, 'Never again,' often had a second or third child, and doted on each one.

The County Hospital, a conglomerate mixture of old and new, had buildings on both sides of the road, and a tower block at one end. Kit didn't leave her car on the main park, which was reserved for hospital staff, but round the corner in a narrow lane, where she usually found a space. There was a line of cars this morning, but still room for hers. She parked, and switched off, and was just getting out when she saw two boys daubing paint over the half a dozen cars parked by the boundary wall. They were so engrossed in what they were doing that they didn't hear her approach, nor see her until she was clear of her own car and yelling at them to stop. They threw the paint can at her; it missed. They ran off, and incensed, she gave chase. They were schoolboys, and she was going to catch them; her temper was good and up.

She had sprinting legs; she set off like the wind, gaining ground with every stride. She could hear her own breathing—quick and controlled. She was near to one of the boys, so near that her feet were right on his heels, so near that her hand trailed his jacket. Then he tripped her—somehow he tripped her—and she uttered a cry, flinging up her arms and falling flat down, sprawled on the dusty road.

She wasn't hurt, just shocked and winded; that much she discovered seconds later when she cautiously rolled over and inspected herself. She sat up. The boys were gone—they weren't even in sight—and for the first time she wondered, as she lurched to her feet, what she would have done if she had caught them, apart from demanding their names, which they would certainly have lied about. The urge to give chase had been a gut reaction and had done no good at all. What a mercy it was that no one had seen her making a fool of herself.

Her hands and the front of her sweater were filthy. She began to dust herself down, then froze as she heard her name being called, for surely she knew that voice. She did—it was Richard's—and, swivelling round, she saw him coming towards her, half walking, half running, and all she could do was stand there and wait for him.

'Are you all right?' He was out of breath.

'Just about!' She managed to smile.

'What happened; did they push you, strike you?' His glance raked her from head to foot.

'I think tripped me, but same difference. . . The ground did the striking,' she joked. She didn't feel like joking, not in the least, but anything was better than stepping towards him and bawling her head off against his shirt. She felt more shaken now than she had at first, and not just from her tumble, either. 'I suppose you saw what happened?' she kept brushing down her dress, not looking at his face but only at his shoes, which were covered in white dust.

'I saw the paint-splashed cars, then you taking off, the boys just ahead. I thought you were all set to catch them, or one of them, anyway.'

'Instead of which—' she managed to smile '—I didn't achieve a thing. I might just as well have turned a blind eye and gone up to the canteen to lunch. Talking of which, I'd better make tracks.' She flipped up her fob watch, relieved to find it was still in one piece, its red minute-hand moving steadily round as usual; it was less shaken up than her.

'Are you sure you're all right?' She felt Richard's hand close over her elbow.

'Quite sure.' They began to walk back towards the line of cars. 'But thank you for coming to my rescue.'

'Oh, for heaven's sake, Kit, what else?' He sounded angry.

'Well, thanks, anyway.' She could feel the grasp of his fingers through her sweater; her thigh brushed his as they walked. Dimly she wondered if he had any idea of the effect he had on her. . . Probably not, but just in case she gave herself away she pulled her arm gently free, and said she could manage, thanks.

So, not touching, but walking alongside, they drew nearer to the cars. Kit could see her Renault at the top end, its chassis sticking out. She had parked it like that in a frantic hurry when she'd rushed to get at the boys. She was surprised to see Richard's blue Peugeot nearest them, as they approached. She hadn't noticed it at all when she'd driven in. Now she could see that it was the only one, bar her own, not vandalised. When she remarked on this, he said it was all down to her. 'If you hadn't arrived in the nick of time, and chased those blighters off, my car would have had the same treatment, being the next one up.'

'Seems I achieved something after all,' she laughed, and looked so relieved and pleased that he felt quite touched.

'All the same,' he said, looking down at her again when they reached the hospital entrance, 'you ought to slip into Casualty, you know and have them check you over.'

'I wouldn't dream of wasting their time,' she scoffed. 'All I need is a wash.'

'No cuts or grazes?'

'Not so much as a scratch.'

'All right, then, I'll let you off.' He looked her straight in the eye as he spoke. If she was lying he'd twig. Their glances held, and this time it was he who looked away first, drawing his brows and staring down at the ground. 'While you're having your wash,' she heard him say, 'I'll go over to Maintenance and see if they can do anything about those cars before the paint dries on.'

'Good idea,' she said shortly, but how very like him that was, for how many men would bother to take any action at all when their own car was sitting there completely clean?

'Before you dash off, Kit——' his hand came out to stop her moving away '—why not forget about the canteen today? Why not come across to the Swan with me and have a ploughman's lunch? Of course, you may be meeting someone, but if not I'd enjoy your company.'

'I'm not meeting anyone, and I'd like to come.' Her

answer came out so pat and so quickly that she couldn't believe she had given tongue to it. She was breaking all the sensible rules, and in a flash of panic was about to retract, and say that she felt she hadn't got time after all, when he came smartly in with,

'See you here in five minutes,' and went off to the maintenance sheds.

In Casualty's cloakrooms she did what she called a passable job on herself, washing her hands, and face, and legs—the latter through her tights—combing her hair, arranging her fringe, stripping off her sweater, which was filthy, and pushing it into her bag. She wasn't, she told herself, tarting up, but no self-respecting girl would dream of going to the Swan Inn, a very upmarket pub, looking as though she'd been dragged behind a plough.

Richard was waiting for her out in the yard. 'You look better already,' he said.

'I should hope so; the dirt's off!'

'Oh, is that what it is?' Looking down at her simply styled wheat-gold hair, at her lashes tipped with the same colour, at her creamy skin, he felt a kind of uplift—a sloughing off of care. Slipping his hand within her bare arm, he steered her through the gates, and across the busy road to the old coaching inn.

They decided, for quickness, to sit up at the bar, and once they'd been served Richard said he was glad of the chance to talk to her alone.

'Oh, dear, that sounds ominous!' Kit's heart was a drum in her ears.

'It's not ominous, but important. It concerns the twins, and the way you look after them.'

'What can you mean by that, I wonder?' Her brown eyes opened wide.

'I mean, if it weren't for you, Josie and I wouldn't be able to go out so often, feeling easy in our minds. Sometimes, though, I've wondered if we impose on you too much, take advantage of you living there, being on the spot. Josie feels the same; I'm quite sure of that,' he added loyally.

Kit broke off a piece of warm, crusty bread, buttered it and said, 'Josie and I understand one another pretty well, you know. Also I've got a tongue in my head, and my name's not Martha. I'd soon speak out if I felt I was being used.'

'I'm glad to hear it,' he said quickly, but the surprise in his eyes goaded her on to tell him that she very often went out. Slightly baffled by her tone, he said, 'Good, that's fine!' then busied himself paying the barman who was handing them their drinks.

They were non-alcoholic drinks, as they were both on duty. A good stiff gin would have been welcome, but fatal, Kit thought ruefully, for she might have been tempted, sorely tempted, to tell Richard, without giving reasons, of course, that she was soon going to leave the Russell Road house. Even without the spur of alcohol she very nearly succumbed, but somehow she managed to hold back, for it would hardly be fair to Jo to go blurting it out pell-mell before she knew herself.

'I go out whenever I want,' she insisted, glancing sideways at Richard. He nodded, and she wondered at herself for labouring the point so much. What was she trying to do, for heaven's sake, give him the impression that she had a string of boyfriends queuing up for dates? True, she was currently going out with a male physio from the hospital. They were both swimming enthusiasts, and used the indoor pool. She had been out with her mother's lodger too, and would probably be asked again. And while two wasn't exactly a queue, it was a satisfactory number, and all she had time and energy for. Midwifery was very hard work.

Looking over the bar counter into the mirror behind the bottles, she could see Richard's and her reflection—her blue dress against his dark suit, her gold head to the right of his jet one. She could see him raising his glass, drinking from it, then setting it down, his shoulder brushing hers. 'I met your mother at the hospital the other day,' he remarked conversationally, and Kit relaxed, for this was a safe subject.

'Mother likes doing her bit,' she responded eagerly, beginning to enjoy her lunch at last.

'Yes, I was visiting a patient when she came in with her trolley of books. As a matter of fact she very nearly ran it over my feet. . . Awkward things, library trolleys; they have a life of their own. Anyway when she was introduced and I heard the name Greenham, I asked if she had a midwife daughter, and that broke the ice at once.'

'It would; she's inclined to go on a bit.'

'Not at all; I enjoyed our chat. We ended up agreeing that midwifery is an élite profession and a highly respected one.'

'I've never regretted taking it up.' Kit felt a glow at his words. 'It was during my RGN training that I finally made up my mind. The obstetrics section interested me, so once I'd registered I went on to do my midder, which meant another eighteen months.'

'During which time you delivered forty babies, palpated a hundred abdomens, postnatally examined a hundred women along with their hundred babies, not to mention assisting at forty complicated births.' He brought this out as a quote from a book, then added smilingly, 'Which would seem to indicate that you like children and involvement with families.'

'Some children, some families!' Kit qualified, returning his smile.

'You'll have children of your own one day.' This came out after a pause. He was looking at his plate, and not at her, and she wondered if he was bored.

'I hope so,' she said, 'if only to be able to identify more with my mothers. I'm just a little tired of being asked, "Have you got any children, Nurse?" and when I tell them no, not yet, getting thrown at me the very true remark of, "Then you can't know what it's like". Somehow or other, there's no reply to that, or I'm hard put to find one.'

'I sympathise.' He laughed a little. 'And to a certain extent you and I are in the same boat, for most patients prefer their doctor to be married—a settled-down type, with a family.'

'Well, you'll soon be that, won't you? September's not very far off,' she said, turning to smile at him, feeling quite pleased with herself for grasping the nettle like that, *and* smiling as well.

He nodded. 'Yes, that's true.' He was looking down into his glass as though it were some kind of crystal ball. He appeared to be lost in thought. 'You've known Josie for a long time, haven't you?' he said at last, just as Kit was beginning to wonder if she might have given offence.

'Since we were five years old,' she told him. 'We

went to the same schools. We were inseparable until Josie married and I went off to the Midlands to train.'

'Yes, that's what I thought. So you'll have known Paul Brett?'

'Why, yes, of course. I was with Jo when she met him. . . I was a bridesmaid at their wedding.' She stopped there, purposely, telling herself to watch out, for she didn't know what Josie had told Richard about Paul. She wouldn't have painted him black, she was sure, for that wouldn't have been very fair. What Kit had seen of Paul Brett she had very much liked. He and Josie had been incompatible largely because of the age gap of fifteen years, which needn't have mattered if Josie hadn't been young for her age, and he over-old for his.

After the divorce he'd had access to the twins, whom he saw whenever he could. He was an international accountant, so was often out of the country, but when he was in it, and if the boys were on holiday he took them off to Oxford to stay with his parents, who doted on them as much as the Telfords did.

'The twins speak of him often.' Richard was clearly bent on gleaning more information about Paul, but Kit still trod carefully.

'Well,' she said slowly, 'he *is* their father, and he takes an interest in them. He's nearly always out of England, though; his job takes him abroad. It's probably that that makes him seem exciting to the boys.'

'Probably, yes.' Richard nodded.

'And Josie tells me,' Kit went on, 'that *you* worked abroad before she knew you, with the World Health Organisation.'

'I did, yes.' His face cleared. 'Out in East Africa.

Now that was an experience, if ever there was one, making the practice of medicine in the UK a doddle in comparison. I've been with my father eighteen months now, and our partnership is working well.'

'I know nurses who've gone abroad,' Kit said. 'I have a friend in Nicaragua, where there are shortages of even the most basic equipment and drugs.'

'A challenge, if ever there was one.'

'Yes.'

'But not one that you want to take up?'

'No way!' Kit shook her head. 'I've only just returned to my roots. This part of the Thames Valley is my favourite part of the world.'

'We'd miss you if you upped and left us now.'

'Thank you for those kind words!' They were the words she wanted to hear, of course, especially coming from him. Yet *if* she left—if, eventually, she found she had to do so—he would be the reason for it. Oh, how complicated things were! She sighed and he heard her. 'Want to go?' He signalled to the barman.

'It's a case of having to, rather than wanting to.' She slid down from her stool.

'Same here. Don't forget your bag.' He looped it over her shoulder, and she moved it in place, aware of his nearness, not daring to look at him. It would be awful if he could read her thoughts, which were in no way professionally linked. But of course he couldn't—she was being silly—for thoughts didn't appear above one's head in graduated bubbles, the way they did in cartoons.

They were soon outside once more, crossing the road to the hospital. There it was, looming in front of them, spreading itself out in blocks. 'I came here in the hope of collecting two reports from Haematology.' Richard looked towards the laboratory block. 'They're very long-winded these days.'

'I expect they're short-staffed,' Kit said.

They turned right into the side-lane. All the same cars were there, but with a difference: they were all spanking clean, not a paint smear to be seen. 'Well, now, will you look at that?' Richard whistled under his breath. 'Maintenance have turned up trumps.'

'All due to you,' Kit said. 'You were the one who bothered to alert them. It was a thoughtful thing to do.'

'Was it?' He sounded surprised.

'Well, *I* thought so. . . I thought it was fabulous!' Then, embarrassed by her praise, she stepped out to cross to her car, neither seeing nor hearing the motor-cyclist roaring in until she was right in his path, until he was only feet away from her, until she was stiffening herself for the impact. . .which must come. . .which must come. Then she felt herself snatched, pulled backwards, dragged and hauled to safety, while the bike roared on, while Richard's voice—for it was he who held her—came angrily into her ear.

'For God's sake, what are you trying to do, scare me half to death?' He was turning her to face him bundling her round, hands tight on her upper arms. She looked up at him, shaken, dazed, saw his face an inch away, then his mouth was on hers in a hard, swift kiss of straining intensity, which stopped her breath and surely her heart, making her legs go weak.

She couldn't believe it had happened, and neither, perhaps, could he. He was white round the mouth as he took her arm and steered her across the lane. 'I'll see you to your car before any more dangers loom!' He was trying to laugh; so was she. 'Give me your keys.' He took them from her, unlocked her car door, and waited while she got in. 'Mind how you go.'

She knew he was peering in at her, but it took all the will-power she had to turn and meet his eyes, which looked wary and troubled, belying the smile which played around his mouth. 'Thank you for the lunch, and for saving me from ending up a mess in the lane.' She managed to say this perfectly steadily, but she needn't have bothered, for someone had called him, and he was going off, lifting a hand in farewell.

It took time for her to fasten her seatbelt and switch her engine on. It took time to move off the precinct and drive steadily through the town. She could still feel the driving pressure of Richard's mouth on hers. He had kissed her like that in the aftermath of shock, and she had kissed him back. She knew she had; she couldn't deny it, least of all to herself. In those flying moments when the bike had raced by, roaring up the lane, emotion had caught them by the throat, and had made them both vulnerable.

All she hoped—fervently hoped—was that she hadn't given herself away. She just prayed that he had no inkling of how she felt about him.

CHAPTER THREE

KIT'S first visit that afternoon was to an Austrian-born expectant mother, who lived in Springbrook Close. Eve Taylor was married to a milkman, whom she had met when he had gone to Salzburg on holiday in the seventies. After sixteen years in England and three children, Eve was still 'foreign' in her ways. She was also a loving wife and mother who, right from the first, had embraced her new country with the enthusiasm she applied to everything.

'I am feeling very well now,' she said, as soon as she saw Kit. She was a big woman, dark-eyed, with strong white teeth that dominated her broad sallow face when she smiled. She was wearing an old-fashioned smock of dark grey, which didn't become her. 'Now, get to the side,' she told the two little girls who were playing in the passage. 'They haf both got colds, so I keep them at home.'

'Much the best,' said Kit, saying hello to the three-year-old boy who was making his way down the stairs with a tabby cat in his arms. There were three kittens belonging to the cat; there was also a collie dog, and a parrot called Beadle, who lived in the sitting-room. Kit had met them all before.

'I am beeg, aren't I, for five month?' Eve said upstairs, as Kit measured the height of her fundus, took a blood-pressure reading, obtained and tested a urine sample, and listened to her heart.

'You're doing splendidly, Eve,' she said at the end of it all. 'As you're a multipara mother—have had other children—you're not too big. You're just a nice size—about right, I'd say.'

'I hope it will be you who come to me when my baby is born.' Eve rebuttoned her smock, and rolled down her sleeve.

'I hope so too.' Kit knew she was booked for a home delivery. Richard, whose patient Eve was, had raised no objection to this. 'You'll be attended by two of us—two midwives—and one of them will be me, if that's my shift, or if I'm on call, but, if I shouldn't be, you know the other midwives, don't you—Tessa, Joyce and Sue?'

'Oh, yes, I know, and I like you all,' Eve said comfortably.

Lovely to have a nature like hers, Kit thought as she left the house some fifteen minutes later, carefully stepping over a toy tractor and a kitten in the hall. Then outside at the gate she met Eve's husband, Bill, just coming in with the dog.

'Is everything all right with Eve?' he asked, restraining the dog, who like his mistress had a welcoming nature. His tail thumped against Kit's legs.

'Couldn't be better, Mr Taylor.' She smiled back into his square, blunt-featured face, allaying the faint anxiety which he obviously couldn't help feeling whenever he saw a nurse walk down the path.

It was a little after four-thirty, and three visits later, when Kit drove to Upper Clements Street to book in the new 'mother', Dinah James, whom Richard had told her about.

She turned out to be small, red-haired and freckled,

and she eyed Kit suspiciously before asking her into the house and through to the sitting-room. Her husband was there, sitting forward on the settee in white bib overalls. He was a self-employed builder and had come home early, as he wanted to be in on the act. 'What are we supposed to call you?' he grunted when Kit introduced herself as midwife Kit Greenham and extended her hand, which was taken, then quickly dropped.

'Most of my mothers call me Kit,' she said. 'It's more friendly and less of a mouthful.'

'In that case, we're Dinah and Bob,' Dinah said promptly, forestalling her husband, who looked as though he was about to object.

Kit tried to break the stiff atmosphere by admiring their loose-covered chairs, and she hit the right note, for even Bob's face brightened a little then.

'Di made them,' he said. 'She's had proper lessons. . . went to evening classes.'

'I run a little business from home, here,' Dinah explained. 'Just curtains and covers—simple things. I don't go in for tailoring.'

'Well, how enterprising,' Kit exclaimed. 'I'm no good at that kind of thing.'

'I've got a workroom upstairs—in the attic, actually. Bob did it up for me, put in a skylight and everything, so all my stuff is out of the way.'

'Brilliant!' Kit was undoing her case, and, feeling a little more accepted into this prickly household, she got down to the business of her visit, bringing out pen and pad. A booking-in history took a long time. There were so many questions that had to be answered; it was worse than a census form. 'I notice,' she said, 'from the letter that Dr Anstey has written to the hospital that you want to be delivered there, but would like shared care.'

'What I would *like*,' Dinah said, looking straight at her husband, 'is not to be having a baby at all!'

Just for a second Kit was thrown, for she hadn't expected that. Richard hadn't given her any indication, but then he might not have known.

'*But*,' Dinah continued, shaking back her hair, 'Bob wants a kid, so I've agreed to go through with it, and I did tell the doctor that I'd have it in hospital, but I dread going there. I've always been afraid of hospitals. I can't help it; I just am. I'd like a home birth, but Bob's against it, and I think he ought to consider my feelings more than he is!' She glared at her husband, who glared back, then looked over at Kit.

'I want it born in hospital, where Di will be safe.' His voice became almost a mutter. He was upset, Kit realised. He was worried about the whole thing—hence his aggressive front.

'Given a normal pregnancy,' she explained, 'Dinah would be safe here. Dr Anstey is a qualified obstetrician, and we have a team of midwives. Still,' she added quickly, seeing Bob's jaw jut, 'as the two of you can't quite decide. . .' she was straining to be tactful '. . .perhaps you would like to think about a domino delivery?'

'What the hell's that?' Bob exclaimed, while Dinah merely looked blank.

'Domino stands for domiciliary in and out,' Kit explained. 'What it actually means is that when the woman goes into labour she contacts her midwife, who comes to her home, monitors her progress, stays with her till she's well advanced, then takes her to hospital where she delivers her in their maternity unit, using their equipment and staff. After the baby is born and the mother has rested, the midwife brings both of them home.'

'So the hospital stay isn't long, then?' Dinah was the first to speak.

'A matter of hours only, just so that the mother can rest. After that the midwife takes over at home and provides continuing care.'

'I could put up with that.' Dinah looked at her husband, who shrugged and said nothing at all. 'Well, say something, can't you?' she snapped at him, and once again the atmosphere was all crossed swords. Dear God, what a couple, Kit thought, sitting there with a bright, enquiring face.

'Perhaps you'd both like to think it over—' she began, but was cut off short.

'No, we wouldn't.' It was Dinah who spoke. 'I'll have the domino thing, and if Bob doesn't like it he can lump it; I'm fed up with arguing!'

Bob laughed; amazingly he laughed, throwing back his head. 'Keep your wig on, Di; don't be so touchy.' He leaned forward and gripped her knee. 'I'll go along with the domino scheme; seems to me it's the best of both worlds. Can you arrange it for us?' He looked at Kit, who nodded and told him she could.

The remainder of the visit proceeded smoothly. Even so it was nearly six before Kit left the house and climbed into her car. As Clements Street was on the Grantford side of Melbridge, she decided to drive to Ford House to sound out her mother about moving home for a time.

Free now of patients and their problems—at least until next day—her mind filled up with Richard, as though thoughts of him had been gathering there, right on its rim, ready to avalanche in. They were chaotic thoughts, so not all made sense, but some of them did—the ones that told her things would simplify once she'd moved out of Russell Road. It wouldn't stop the way she felt about him. . .not for a very long time. . . but she would see less of him, which would make the situation endurable.

She found her mother in the garden planting hydrangeas, a bag of peat at her side and Daisy, her West Highland terrier, helping her dig the holes. 'Kit. . . why, *darling*!' She got to her feet with surprising agility for a lady of sixty-six years. 'I thought you were coming at the weekend. . .don't tell me that's off!'

'No, Mummy, nothing like that.' The two women kissed. 'But I was fairly near when I finished my shift, so thought I'd drop in.'

'Quite right.' Mrs Greenham slipped off her gardening gloves. 'Let's go into the house, shall we? I can do with a rest.' So in they went, along the flagged path, the sun dappling the stones, and Daisy circling in front of them, excited by Kit's coming, and by the prospect of her evening meal, which she had at about six o'clock.

'Have you eaten?' Mrs Greenham asked as she washed and dried her hands in the fitted kitchen, which she'd only just had installed.

'No, but I haven't come to eat.' Kit picked Daisy up in her arms. 'I've come to ask if I can move in for a time—come home to live, just until I can find something nearer the midwives' base.'

Mrs Greenham swung round, 'For goodness' sake, child, you don't have to ask! This is your home. Of *course* you can come. Isn't the arrangement with Josie working? I suppose,' she went on, before Kit could answer, 'that she's been taking advantage all round. That's her way, you know; she was always like that, but you could never see it.'

'She hasn't been taking advantage, Mum.' Kit put Daisy back on the floor. 'It's been give and take all the way; there's been no problem there.'

'Then why are you leaving? Is it the twins? Small children can be trying, I know.'

'It's not the twins; I love them both.'

'Yes, I rather thought you did; they're grand little boys. So what is it, my darling? It's unlike you to chop and change.'

Looking over at her mother, at her lined, pretty face, at her greying blonde hair, at her brown eyes, wide-spaced like her own, at her generous curving mouth, Kit was tempted, sorely tempted to confide in her, yet something held her back. There was a wide gap between mothers and daughters, the chasm of years and differing values, which sadly but inevitably eschewed close confidences. So she didn't explain—she couldn't—but neither did she lie. All she said was, 'I can't tell you the reason, but I know it's the best thing to do.'

Mrs Greenham nodded, 'All right, then, darling; that's good enough for me. Come when you like; your room's always ready. Why only the other day I bought a new goose-down duvet, so I must have had some inkling or premonition that something lovely was about to happen, like this.'

'Thanks,' Kit said, and felt choked for a moment, while her mother turned her back and started talking about a casserole, saying there was plenty if Kit wanted to change her mind and stay.

'Having Andrew here makes me cook more.' She bent down to the oven. '*And* I enjoy it—both the cooking and the eating; I shall soon start putting on weight.'

'Is Andrew here at home now?' Kit had forgotten him for the moment.

'Yes, in the breakfast-room, marking books. I don't use that room, as you know. It gives him an extra sitting-room—apart from his bedroom, I mean. He's so easy, Kit, so quiet; I hardly know he's around. Now, darling, you haven't told me—*can* you stop for a meal?'

'No, Josie will have something ready, and she and I have to talk. I'll ring you tomorrow—Wednesday—then we'll discuss when I can move in.'

'We'll discuss when you'll be *coming home*,' Mrs Greenham corrected, straightening up as a knock on the door brought Andrew Macauley Gordon into their midst—a tall, broad man with dun-coloured hair, vivid blue eyes, and a way of standing perfectly upright without a hint of a slouch. He was neat too, for such a big man. There was nothing awry; even his gorgeous Aran sweater hung level all the way round. But he looked, Kit thought, a little abstracted, as though he hadn't divorced his mind from the task of marking books. He blinked, got Kit into focus, then smiled unstintingly. 'Hello, Kit, I thought I heard voices.'

'Hello, Andrew, how are things?'

'Not so bad on the whole. You're all right, are you?'

'Fine, yes, but just about to go.' She looked at the steaming casserole. 'I'm holding up your meal.'

'Please don't go on my account.' He bent to fondle Daisy. Her paws were black with peat, and Kit warned him not to let her jump up.

'Kit is moving back home for a time,' Mrs Greenham remarked, crashing cutlery down on a tray for taking into the dining-room. Andrew reached for it, and raised it.

'Oh, really. . .? When's this to be?' As he turned to Kit, tray in hand, she couldn't fail to see that he looked pleased at the prospect, and she drew a small breath of relief. Ford House wasn't his home, it was hers, but, even so, he might not have been all that keen to have his ménage with her mother disturbed.

'I'm not completely sure when,' she said, 'but as soon as possible.'

'Oh, well, that's splendid news, and if you need any help with all the transference let me know.' He opened the door with his foot, smiling goodbye over his shoulder and going out into the hall.

'He's a thoroughly nice man,' Mrs Greenham whispered once he was out of earshot. 'He's done well to get a post at the Dartings. Georgina told me there were loads of applicants, and Andrew was first choice.'

Georgina Gordon was Andrew's mother, and a friend of Mrs Greenham's, which was how he came to be at Ford House and not in conventional digs.

'Good for him. As you say, he's done well.' Kit picked her bag up off the floor.

'His fiancée threw him over.' Mrs Greenham's voice dropped even lower. 'It was about a year ago, I think. According to Georgina, that's what made him seek a complete change.'

Kit already knew this, from Andrew himself, but didn't tell her mother so, just kissed her goodbye and said she would ring as soon as she'd fixed things with Jo.

The worst of the traffic rush was over as she drove swiftly back through Grantford towards the outskirts of Melbridge, using the ring road. When she moved she was going to have a longer drive to her base, but not *all* that much longer, she quickly assured herself. Once in Russell Road she found herself slowing long before she was near the house. It was one of those times when it was better to travel than to arrive, she thought wryly, as she eased the car into the garage at last.

The television was on; she could hear one of the advertisement jingles once she was in the house and had started up the stairs. Josie heard her and called out, 'Poor old thing, aren't you late? The boys are in bed, but can you look in on them? They won't go to sleep unless——'

'Will do.' Through the sitting-room doorway Kit could see Jo on the settee. She had washed her hair and was blow-drying it, holding it up in the air. Daniel's voice came from the bedroom.

'Come and say goodnight.'

'An' say goodnight, Kit,' echoed Harry, never far behind his brother.

When Kit entered their bedroom they were sitting bolt upright, looking expectant, fair hair licked flat, pyjama collars rucked, duvets pushed down to their waists. 'Read to us, Kit. Read us *Black Beauty*, the part where he goes——'

'No, Daniel, not tonight.' Kit made her voice firm. 'I want to talk to Mummy, and you ought to be asleep.'

'We waited for you,' they chanted, but consented to lie down at last.

'We always do,' Harry yawned. They were on the borders of sleep, which was just as well, for what they said made Kit feel terrible. Still, she couldn't change her mind now, could she? Not even for their sakes. Kissing them both, adjusting their blinds, leaving the door ajar, she went downstairs exactly as she was, still in her uniform.

Josie had turned off the television, and was filing her nails. 'Supper is the last of the joint and some salad. Is that enough?' she asked.

'Plenty.' The last thing Kit wanted was food; the thought of it sickened her.

'You look done in.' Josie's glance was concerned. 'Let's have a drink before we start.' She got to her feet then perched on the arm of the couch in front of Kit. 'There's nothing wrong, is there?' Her engagement ring flashed fire as she pushed her hair back from her face. It was that more than her enquiry that started Kit off.

'Look, Jo,' she said gently, looking straight back at her friend, 'I've been thinking for a week or two now that I ought to go home to live. Mother would like it, and you'll be moving out soon, anyway. It's been smashing here, and I've loved it, but. . .now's the time to go.'

'*What* did you say?' Josie stared, wide-eyed, dropping the file in her lap.

'I want to move out, to live at home,' Kit repeated, as Josie jumped up.

'I can't believe I'm hearing this!'

'I'm really sorry, Jo.'

'Then you *do* mean it?' She was incredulous, flushed.

'Yes, I do.'

'But what have I *done*?'

'Nothing, absolutely nothing.'

'Then why. . .for God's sake, *why*? You've not lived at home for absolute yonks! You can't want that kind of scene now!' She made home sound like the worst kind of refuge, which Kit had never felt it was.

'I feel I'd like to move there; it just seems right.'

'And never mind how *I* feel. . . That doesn't count at all!'

'Oh, Josie!'

'It's the twins, I suppose.' She gnawed at her lip. 'I've been pushing them on you too much. Richard said I was being unfair; taking advantage. So if it's that, if it's them, perhaps we can come to some sort of—'

'It's not the twins; it's nothing to do with the boys. I shall miss them when I go. I just simply want a change; I just simply want to go home.'

'Do you really *mean* it?' She was still incredulous.

'I really and truly do.'

'So much for friendship!' Josie all but spat out the words.

'Oh, for heaven's sake, Jo.' Kit was almost glad to feel a rush of anger. 'You can perfectly well do without me here. It was never, in any case, going to be forever. . . You'll soon be married and off yourself!'

'You needn't move out, not even then. We had all that out, remember? I told you you could stay till the house was sold. It would have been ideal, having someone on the spot when the agent brought viewers round.'

'You won't be all that far away yourself, in Palmerstone Drive.'

'Oh, all right, be like that!' Josie turned her back, and began picking threads from one of the cushions. 'So, when are you going?' she asked.

'I thought at the weekend, if that's all right, but I'll pay my full month's rent.' It might have been better not to have mentioned money—at least, not just then—for Josie wheeled round, looking furious, angry tears filling her eyes.

'Oh, for goodness's sake, Kit, I don't want your rent! I'm not hard up! It was you who insisted on a rental basis; I've always hated it! And I don't believe what you say about Mrs Greenham wanting you home. Why, only a few weeks back, when I met her in the town, she said how pleased she was that I was putting you up!'

'Since then,' Kit said, feeling caught out, 'she's taken in a p.g.'

'Well, I know that, don't I. . .the blue-eyed Scot. Perhaps——'

'He makes extra work.' She felt even more guilty when she said that, for Andrew didn't make work; he helped, and her mother liked having him. She had resorted to lying now.

The click of a car door closing turned both girls to the window. Richard, the cause of all the trouble, was coming across the lawn. Josie flew to the door as though catapulted there. Kit waited by the window, leaning on the sill, feeling sick, feeling trapped. She could hardly escape to her room, nor even to the kitchen, for she'd meet them both in the hall. Richard hadn't been expected this evening, so his plans must have changed. She could hear him greeting Josie, 'hear' a small silence, which meant they were kissing, then in they came, Josie slightly in front, talking about his meeting having finished earlier than he'd thought.

'Hi, there.' He smiled at Kit no differently from usual, but their eye contact was glancing, as he turned to Josie and said, 'Kit and I met at lunchtime, at the hospital. She saved my car from being daubed by vandals; she chased them up the lane, and would have caught them if—'

'She's leaving, moving out,' Josie broke in, clearly not interested in cars and vandals and lunchtime meetings. What did she care about those? 'She's going home to live at Grantford with her mother; she's just told me so. It was such a shock, so out of the blue! Tell her she mustn't go!'

Richard's eyes were on Kit; she could feel them boring into her back. She was half turned away, moving some books off the arm of a chair. Not until she was seated did he say, still standing, looking down at her, 'I'm sure Kit knows what she wants, Jo. It's not for us to interfere.'

'But to be going back *home*!' Josie pulled at his hand, and he sat by her on the settee. 'She's never lived at home—well, not for ages—and to want to go so soon. . .this weekend! It's as though she can't wait, can't wait to get away. It's as though I've upset her, or someone else has—'

'Oh, don't be ridiculous!' Kit felt herself going rigid as she sat. The ticking of the clock became over-loud, and as she moved her foot she kicked the pile of books over again, spilling them into the hearth. Picking them up gave her something to do.

'Perhaps she's fallen in love,' Josie went on, and once more Kit froze. '*I* think she's fallen for that groovy Scotsman her mother has just taken in. He teaches history at the Dartings, but he's not one of those learned types, not a swot, by any means. I met him one night when he brought her home after a concert at his school. After all, there has to be *some* good reason for her going home to Mum!'

She wasn't teasing so much as taunting. Not that that bothered Kit; she was only too relieved that Josie hadn't stumbled on the truth. Aware that both she and Richard were waiting for her to react, she smiled and said, 'How did you guess?' and looked mysterious.

The telephone began to ring in the hall, and Josie jumped up. 'It'll be for me, probably my parents. I was expecting them to call.' She was gone in a flash, closing the door behind her as she went, closing it firmly till it clicked, leaving Kit and Richard alone.

At first neither spoke; there was just the clock ticking its head off again, and the intermittent mumble of Josie's voice in the hall. Then Kit rose. 'I've not eaten yet, so I'll take myself kitchenwards.' She smiled forcedly at Richard who, already on his feet, gave every appearance of stopping her getting to the door.

'Look, this has to be said, so I'll get it over with.' His embarrassment was plain, so was his determination to speak before Josie came back in. 'If your sudden decision to take yourself off has anything to do with what happened at lunchtime, you don't have to go, you know. What I'm trying to say, trying to tell you, is that it won't happen again. I wouldn't like you to think——'

'There's no need to explain,' Kit cut in quickly, 'and I don't think anything. There's nothing between you and me; we both know that. My decision isn't sudden, either; it's been brewing for some time, and Andrew *does* have something to do with it—Josie was right about that. I'm looking forward to living at home and seeing more of him. Sometimes it's almost a holiday to go out with someone *un*-medical!'

'Oh, well, that's all right, then,' he smiled, but she glimpsed the surprise in his eyes; not that she was able to meet them for long, for her statement was speckled with lies.

'Now that we've cleared that up,' she said, 'I'll go and get my supper.'

'Of course, sorry.' He opened the door, and they saw Josie in the hall. She had finished on the phone, and was standing there, deep in thought.

'I'll take my tray upstairs, leave you in peace.' Kit made her way to the kitchen.

'All right, yes; we can talk later.' Josie, all smiles again, moved towards Richard. 'That was Dad,' Kit heard her say.

A few minutes later, carrying food that she had little appetite for up the stairs to her bed-sit, she could see the engaged couple through in the sitting-room, merged on the couch. They had forgotten her already, which was natural enough. Even so, their unconcern was very hard to take. Anger flared like a match in Kit, and she had to restrain herself from throwing the tray, contents and all, over the top of the polished banisters, just to scare them out of their wits.

CHAPTER FOUR

IN THE end the move from Melbridge to Grantford went off very well. There was nothing heavy, like furniture, to shift, only clothes and odds and ends. Josie helped Kit bring these downstairs and load them into the Renault the following Friday morning, after she'd taken the boys to school.

Once her initial annoyance had died, Josie was resigned to Kit's going. 'Grantford is only minutes away, so we can still see one another nearly as much,' she insisted, watching her friend get in the car.

'Of course we can,' Kit promised, feeling, now that she was actually off, a tremendous sense of relief. It was going to feel strange at home, she knew that, and she would miss seeing the twins on a daily basis, which she had always enjoyed. Daniel and Harry knew she wouldn't be there when they came home from school. Josie had explained the situation to them, and they had looked rather solemn-eyed, but their mother was the firmament in their world, and, so long as she was around, other people could come and go. They were adaptable little boys.

At the Grantford end Mrs Greenham welcomed her daughter with open arms. Daisy, catching the excitement, tore round the lawn like a motorbike, and when Andrew Gordon got in that evening he presented both women with a bouquet of mixed carnations and a bottle of *rosé* wine. 'But surely it's a celebration,' he said, waving aside Mrs Greenham's cries of, 'Oh, you shouldn't have, Andrew, but what a lovely surprise!'

During the weeks that followed Kit found the extra journey she had to make far from ideal, but the reason for it was soon paying dividends, for she saw Richard far less often, which *had* to mean that her feelings for him would lessen too, for nothing, she told herself, survived on nothing. She had to get over him.

Josie and she usually met on Wednesdays, which, unless Kit was on call, was the evening she went to Russell Road to catch up on all the news. Naturally enough, Richard often came into their conversation, and one night Josie outlined their wedding plans.

'It'll be a register office affair,' she said, 'so we needn't fix anything yet. The Ansteys want a family luncheon at the Bridge Hotel, so we'll settle for that, and it *will* be just family—my parents, and Richard's, and the twins, of course. Then there'll be you and Andrew and your mother. I couldn't possibly leave you out.'

'If you go on adding extras, you'll soon swell the numbers, Jo,' Kit said, wishing that she could be the one to be left off the list.

'I couldn't get married without you there.'

'I shan't let you down.'

'It'll be a bit different from the first time, won't it?' Josie was looking back, so was Kit—back eight years to the day Paul Brett had taken Josephine Margaret Telford to be his wedded wife. Josie had been a sensational bride—a fairy princess, no less—her flaxen hair streaming down her back, her slimness emphasised by her tight-waisted taffeta gown that whispered when she walked. Paul Brett had been pretty sensational too—black-bearded and brilliant-eyed. 'My handsome pirate', Josie had used to call him, but that was long ago.

'Kit, you do like Andrew, don't you?' Josie was curious.

'Yes, I do; we get along fine.' Kit smiled straight back at her.

'So something may come of it?'

'Stranger things have happened!' Kit laughed, and changed the subject. It was true; she liked Andrew very much, but friends was all they were, and all they ever would be, which suited them both. She could hardly admit this to Josie, for she had led her to believe that Andrew was the prime reason for her moving back home. It was small wonder that Josie was curious, and small wonder, too, that she was going to ask Andrew to her wedding as though Kit and he were a pair.

During the second week in June Kit paid another visit to Dinah James. At nine weeks, still in her first trimester, she was having one or two problems, not the least of them being nausea, which was making her miserable. 'Most women,' Kit explained to her, 'feel better after the third month, but you can help yourself to a certain extent by having small, dry meals, sucking glucose sweets, even sipping aerated water—the fizzy element will make you burp and give temporary relief.'

'Charming, I'm sure!' Dinah pulled a face. 'And I'm going through all this to have a baby I don't want. . . never wanted to conceive.'

'You'll feel differently about that when you feel better in yourself.'

'You be me!'

'I wouldn't mind if the circumstances were right.'

'That's easy to say.' Dinah reached for her workbox, scowling across at Kit.

She was hand-sewing a curtain hem in a colourful Liberty material. Stopping briefly to admire it, telling her to be careful when using the attic stairs, Kit left the house and went on to another woman suffering from cramp in her legs.

'It grips me in the early morning, Nurse. I wake up with this shocking pain in each calf, and I have to get out of bed and walk around. Even then it's ages before it goes. The other midwife said to eat some yoghurt, or have a milk drink last thing at night, but I'm not very keen on dairy foods. I don't even like cheese very much.'

'I'll get a prescription from your doctor for calcium tablets.' Kit jotted this down in her book, remembering as she did so that she also needed a prescription for Mrs Reynolds of Bray Close, for support stockings, due to varicose veins.

She decided she would try to catch Richard that evening before he started surgery, and in spite of all her resolutions she couldn't help feeling a thrust of excitement at the prospect of seeing him, if only for a minute or two.

She found him in his surgery, talking to his father—Dr Edward Anstey. They turned round to face her as she entered, and she marked the family resemblance. When Richard turned sixty he would look like his father—tall, spare and grey-haired, with an air of distinguishment that was showing even now.

'I'm just going, my dear; he's all yours.' Dr Edward Anstey looked with pleasure at the bright-haired young midwife standing in the doorway, her dark eyes fixed on Richard, figure trim in her blue cotton dress. 'I don't know how you manage to look so cool on an evening like this. Me, now, I'm sweltering,' he smiled, grinding back the sliding door of his adjoining surgery and passing through.

'What can I do for you?' Richard waved her to a chair, reaching for his white coat and dragging it on, scarcely glancing Kit's way. He wasn't over-pleased to see her, that was obvious, but his scarcely perceptible rudeness had the instantaneous effect of putting her on her mettle and quelling her nervousness.

'I'm sorry to come at such a bad time, but I won't hold you up more than I need.' Her voice was as cool as her appearance, which his father had commented on.

'The timing is OK.' He sounded more conciliatory, even apologetic.

'I just need two prescriptions, that's all.' She passed the details over the desk, not looking at him, just pushing his pad and pen nearer to his hand.

'Thank you.' He looked at her again, but she was fastening her case, her sepia lashes lying in crescents on her cheeks.

He was signing the prescriptions when the door opened to admit one of the receptionists, balancing a tray of tea, which she set down on the desk. There were two cups, Kit saw, feeling awkward all over again, for the second cup sat there like a hint to Richard to ask her to stay to tea.

'Here you are, then, signed and sealed.' He passed the scripts over the desk, catching her eye and saying, 'Sorry I snapped at first, but today has been one of those days; you know how it is.'

'I certainly do, and it doesn't matter.' It was impossible then not to return his smile in full measure, when just for a moment—all over again for Kit—time stood still.

'Shall I pour, or will you?' He was looking at the tray.

'Does that mean I'm invited to tea?'

'Of course, what else?'

'Then I'll pour.' She lifted the chunky pot, willing her hand not to shake and spurt tea all over the tray. It didn't; it was steady; control was all. Well done, Kit! Now for the milk; that was fine too. What had she worried about?

'How are things working out for you, now that you're living at home?' he asked conversationally, dropping two sugar lumps into his cup.

'They're working well on all fronts. In fact, better than I thought.' She watched his spoon going round and round, making little whorls in his cup.

'Good.' They began to drink simultaneously, neither looking at the other. 'You're much missed at Russell Road,' Richard ventured at last.

'Oh, am I?' Their eyes met.

'Yes.' His stare was prolonged.

'Well,' Kit said, flushing a little, 'I miss Josie, of course, *and* the twins, although I usually manage to see them one day a week. Nothing goes on the same for ever,' she finished in a rush.

He agreed that it didn't, and in an attempt to get back to professional matters, she told him that one of his patients had missed her last three clinic appointments. 'It's Mrs Hilsdon of Markerstone Avenue. She says she doesn't feel she needs to go as I see her regularly at home. I've pointed out that she'd benefit by meeting other mothers at the clinic, but so far have met with little response.'

'Mrs Hilsdon?' Richard got up and went to the filing-cabinet. 'Now she, if I remember rightly, is in her thirty-fourth week. I'm seeing her tomorrow at evening surgery.' He was reading her notes. 'There are no special problems, are there, anything I should know?'

'A degree of stress incontinence, which she feels self-conscious about. I think that may be why she's reluctant to come to the clinic,' Kit said.

'Could be.' Richard leafed through her papers, his back turned towards Kit. His starched white coat was creased from having been hung up by its loop. His neck and head rose out of it, the latter slightly bent, his hair, jet-black and flat, trying to curl at the nape. But it didn't do to let her thoughts stray into forbidden zones, so she looked away quickly, getting up from the desk and setting the tea-tray to the side.

Outside in the communal waiting area patients were starting to arrive. They could hear the scrape of chairs, an occasional cough, the wailing of a child. Richard slammed the cabinet drawer shut, heaving an audible sigh. 'As this is Wednesday I suppose you're off to Josie's,' he said, walking to the door, then stopping to pick up a paper-clip from the floor.

'I am,' she replied, 'but really only to pop in and out this evening. 'I've got a special Parentcraft meeting, to be held later on, so that husbands and partners will be able to attend.'

'I'm aware of that,' Richard said, opening the door. 'My father was going to show some slides depicting a birth.'

'That'll be the main attraction. We'll probably have

a full house.' Kit laughed, then quickly sobered. 'Richard, did you say he *was* going to show them? Don't tell me he's changed his mind!'

'He hasn't changed his mind in the way that you mean,' Richard assured her, 'but he's been asked to chair a meeting at the hospital—an important meeting to do with their open day to be held in September. He didn't know till this afternoon, so he's asked me to step into the breach.'

'To show the slides?' Kit's eyes widened, while her brows rose into her fringe.

'I'm quite capable. I *have* done it before!' He was laughing at her. Well, of course he was, and of course he'd done it before.

'I'm sorry; I didn't mean to imply——'

'What time do you want me there? It's your meeting, and I don't need to be in at the start. What time will you have finished your talk and discussion?'

'By eight o'clock; I'll time it for then. . .pregnant ladies, especially those in the third trimester, can't be expected to concentrate for long.'

'Right, then, eight o'clock it is.' He opened the door for her, then said, just before she passed into the throng outside, 'You take your job very seriously, don't you?'

'Is there any other way?' she asked, surprised at the comment, meeting his gaze head-on.

'For people like you and me, maybe not.' He shrugged his shoulders and laughed, but he didn't sound amused, nor look it either; worry dwelled in his eyes. She longed to ask him what was wrong, but managed to stop herself. That was Josie's prerogative, wasn't it. . .to soothe his cares away? Richard the man, Kit told herself stoutly, is nothing to do with me.

'Never mind, press on,' she said flippantly. 'See you at eight o'clock.'

He watched her go, then, mindful of the time, he went back into his room, pressed the buzzer for his first patient, and greeted him when he came in.

Two hours later, back at the centre, Kit got ready for the meeting, explaining to the women and husbands and boyfriends who were filing in that the chairs had to be in rows and set close together so that everyone would be able to get a good view of the screen.

Once they were all in, and seated, and the room was packed to the doors, she told them that Dr Richard Anstey would be showing the slides. 'But first,' she went on, 'you've got to put up with me for half an hour. If you remember, we're going to discuss the pain of labour this evening, and how best to cope with it. . . Every woman varies, of course. Now, there are several of you here who have had babies. Would anyone like to tell us how you coped. . .how you dealt with it all?'

'I walked around leaning on things, and swearing my head off,' one girl said, and others agreed that they'd done exactly the same. Two others said they'd lain in a warm bath; another said she'd practised yoga. Several said they just 'got on with it' and prayed for it to end.

'Would anyone like to tell me what she's most afraid of?' Kit asked, and once again the replies were various and came from all sides. . . 'That I'll be hideous in that region afterwards, and that my husband will go off me. . .' 'That the baby will die before he gets born. . .' 'That my insides will be pulled out.'

Kit was dealing with these and other fears voiced when Richard arrived, walking quietly up the side of the room and sitting down near the front. She saw him and couldn't be unaware of him, but wasn't put off her stroke, partly because she knew her subject, but also because his presence was uncritical, very nearly unobtrusive. He simply sat there at the end of the row as part of the audience.

When the time came for him to show the slides he needed no introduction. As he made his way to the top of the room and stood beside Kit, all eyes were upon him, and there was a heartening response when he said, 'Good evening,' and explained about his father not being able to come. 'So I shall be showing the slides which depict the progress of labour from the end of the first stage through the second stage to the actual moment of birth. I shall show them slowly with plenty of time between each one for questions or discussion of any aspects that might not be clear to you. This, of course, is the great advantage of slides over a film. No one likes to interrupt a film, and interruptions in the form of queries are what Midwife Greenham and I are here for.' He looked at Kit as he said this, and instantly she felt in unity with him. He made her feel important. He's an absolutely super guy, she thought as she started to draw the curtains to darken the room, and roll down the white screen facing the rows of chairs.

There were a dozen slides in all, the first showing a red-haired young woman being propped into a sitting position on an obstetric table. There was a midwife on either side of her, and a hovering medical student, while at her head a gowned-up young man was gripping her hand, with a face very nearly as contorted as her own.

Several questions were asked after each of the first few slides, but after the tenth, when the baby's head had crowned, after the eleventh, when his face was visible, and after the twelfth, when he lay with flailing fists between his mother's legs, there was a pin-drop quiet, as though the audience was too scared or too spellbound to utter a word.

'How long did it all take, from start to finish?' was the first question to break the silence, but before either Kit or Richard could answer there was the sound of a chair crashing over at the back of the room, followed by the thud of a body hitting the floor, and a shriek of 'Dom! It's my Dom. . .it's Dom!' People tried to turn round, and some shot to their feet. A man sniggered and said, 'He's passed out. . .not enough bottle!'

'It's no joke to faint, nothing to laugh at!' Kit was hurrying to the spot, pushing her way through the rows of chairs. Someone pushed the curtains back.

'It's not a faint.' The man's wife was distraught. 'He's having a fit!' Not that Kit needed to be told this; one glance was enough. Dominic Gregson was in the tonic stage of a grand mal seizure—limbs extended, muscles rigid, face deeply cyanosed. As she knelt beside him he passed swiftly into the clonic stage, limbs wildly threshing, breathing stertorous.

By this time Richard was beside her, helping mothers and husbands and partners to move back, giving the convulsing man on the floor enough space to ensure that he wouldn't injure himself against chairs. Kit managed to slip a rolled-up handkerchief in between his teeth, but he had already bitten his tongue, causing blood to ooze out of his mouth.

'You see to Mrs Gregson; I'll look after him,' Richard muttered against Kit's ear, and she did as he said, reassuring Pat Gregson and one or two others as well. For the last thing we want, she thought grimly, is half a dozen shock births.

Pat was calming down now that Dominic was coming out of the fit. 'He hasn't had a fit for a long time,' she said. 'Not for nearly a year—not since I started the baby, anyway. Is he going to be all right?'

'Yes, I'm sure he is.' Kit persuaded her to sit down again. Her husband now appeared to be in a faint, but quickly came out of it. As he tried to sit up, looking dazed, Richard supported him.

'You've had a fit, Dominic. You've nipped your tongue, maybe bruised your legs, but you'll be all right. . . You've come out of it well. . .just sit where you are for a bit.'

Kit, again at Richard's suggestion, was hooking back the doors, and dismissing the meeting. 'We were nearly finished, weren't we?' she said. There was a murmur of assent and possibly of relief as well, as everyone filed out.

Pat Gregson was sitting on a chair, leaning well back, touching the top of her husband's head as he lay propped up by the wall. He had recovered quickly. His colour had returned, and he wanted to go home, and after Richard had examined him he agreed that this would be best. 'We came by bus,' Pat said, 'but perhaps we should sport a taxi.'

'Better still, I'll run you home. Perhaps you'll come with us?' The latter remark was addressed to Kit, who agreed at once. It would be better if she went as well, just in case Pat Gregson, in her thirtieth week, should have an adverse reaction to seeing her husband in a grand mal fit.

All was well, however, half an hour later, when they

left the young couple in their flat in Eastern Terrace, on the outskirts of the town. 'It was most likely those damn slides that set him off,' Richard said, as they drove back to the centre, so that Kit could pick up her car. 'It's the flashing on and off effect that often triggers a fit.'

'He's not your patient; you didn't know he was an epileptic. You can't possibly blame yourself,' Kit said stoutly, covering her ears as an ambulance sirened by. It was nine-thirty and getting dark; the headlamps of oncoming traffic streamed intermittently into the car, and she saw Richard's face in snatches only, his glasses hiding his eyes.

'Even so. . .' he sounded hoarse and tired '. . .it's not a good feeling to know I may have made the poor chap ill. I've suggested he sees his GP tomorrow, in case his drugs need adjusting.'

'It's Dr Foxley.'

'Yes, I know. He's Josie's and the twins' GP too.'

'And mine.'

'He's an excellent doctor.'

'Yes, he certainly is.'

Their conversation, little more than spasmodic, ceased altogether as Richard concentrated on getting the car into the swirl of traffic at the roundabout. . . never an easy task. Once this was accomplished they were only minutes from the health centre building, square and white on its corner site, the police station opposite.

Richard braked and stopped. 'Thanks for coming with me.' He turned his face to Kit's.

'Oh, that's all right; it didn't take long.' She could see him plainly now, see his eyes, which, without his glasses, had an unguarded appeal. She could hear the faint sound of his breathing, or perhaps it was her own. In a rush of panic she made to unslot her belt and met his hand bent on the same errand, and instantly a drive of feeling shot through her, so sharp it was nearly pain, so keen that it made her gasp and say over-loudly all in a rush; 'It's not easy to find these fiddly things in the dark!'

'No, it's not.' He moved. He was getting out; so was she, with equal swiftness. 'I'll see you to your car.' He coughed as he walked round to join her at the kerb.

'There's no need, Richard.' She couldn't look at him. 'I mustn't hold you up, and I must get a move on myself, or Mother and Andrew will be sending out a search-party for me. . .you know how it is.'

'Yes, of course.' He stepped back a pace.

'Those slides helped a lot,' she added a little more warmly, feeling she'd been abrupt. 'I think everyone learned from them, in the right sort of way. You killed off a lot of bogies and old wives' tales for most of my. . .most of *our* mothers tonight.'

'I'm glad of that.' When he smiled she felt her knees going slack again.

'Night, then.' She turned away.

'Goodnight, Kit, drive carefully.' He watched her pull off the forecourt, waved to her as she passed, then got back into his car, glancing briefly at the passenger seat beside him that held her presence still.

CHAPTER FIVE

KIT's days off fell at the weekend again during the last part of June. They also coincided with a mini heatwave, the weathermen predicting temperatures in the mid-eighties, 'but cooler on the coast'. On Saturday morning Mrs Greenham, rising early, decided to get out the garden furniture and serve breakfast on the patio.

Kit, coming downstairs in a sleeveless top and swirling cotton skirt, found Andrew already out there, eating cereal, her mother hovering behind him with his boiled egg and toast.

'What a good idea to have it out here.' She pulled out a chair and sat down, smiling at both him and her mother, noticing how the pale blue of Andrew's sports shirt reflected in his eyes.

'It's going to be a scorcher.' He passed her the sugar, watched her sprinkling it on her grapefruit, then tentatively asked, 'Have you got anything planned for this morning?'

'Oh, Kit,' Mrs Greenham broke in, 'could you possibly do some shopping for me—the boring weekend sort? I know it's a chore, darling, so say if you can't, but the thing is I promised to pop down the road and see old Mrs Bowman. She's just out of hospital after her hip replacement, and is feeling a little low.'

'Course, no problem.' Kit closed an eye as a spurt of juice hit it.

Andrew was decapitating his egg with the deftness he

applied to everything, then he laid down his knife and said, 'I'll take you shopping, if you like, Kit. We could use my car. I'm actually going into Melbridge; I've two houses I want to view. The particulars look quite promising, so perhaps we could do the shopping first, here in Grantford, and go on from there.'

'Why, yes, fine.' Kit reached for the toast. 'But isn't this a new idea, Andrew—I mean, to be buying a house? I thought you wanted to rent a flat.'

'I did, but I've changed my mind. I've been having second thoughts. I feel it would be better to pay interest on a mortgage than fork out on rent, and if I go for a house I may be able to let part of it. Prices are at rock-bottom just now. I feel it's the time to strike.'

'Oh, how sensible!' Mrs Greenham sounded approving, yet downcast at the same time. 'We shall miss you.'

Andrew laughed. 'I've not gone yet,' he said. 'Finding the right property may take a very long time.'

'It may not; it's a buyer's market.' Kit felt a twinge of envy. How lovely to be able to think in terms of buying a house, becoming its owner, doing with it whatever one willed or wished, coming and going as one pleased.

She wondered as they completed the shopping then motored on to Melbridge if they would run into Josie, for one of the houses Andrew wanted to view was a villa-type one at the top of Russell Road. They collected the keys from Crogers the agents, and were told that as both properties were empty they could look around on their own.

The first house was hopeless—damp and dilapidated, smelling of mildew and mice—but the old-fashioned one in Russell Road had distinct possibilities, with its big, airy rooms and bay windows, and grey slate roof. Kit could see that Andrew liked it, and tried to make him like it more. After all, she reasoned, he couldn't live at Ford House for ever. 'With these two reception rooms downstairs,' she said, 'and three good bedrooms up, you'd have no trouble in letting part of it if you wished. You could let to someone like yourself, who was out all day.'

'And I could walk to the Dartings from here.' He was looking out of the window.

'Well, exactly,' Kit said, 'and you'd save on petrol.' They could see the school from where they were standing, see its bell tower and clock rising up behind the jagged teeth of the old abbey ruins. 'And it's an advantage,' Kit added slowly, 'to be near one's place of work.'

'You're right, of course.' He turned round. 'It deserves consideration.' He began to pace up and down the room, weighing the situation with true Scottish caution—not that Kit blamed him for that. Buying a house was a serious business, and couldn't be rushed. 'I'll make an offer for it, see how far I get,' he said, as they walked to the gate. He was excited—Kit could see that—so perhaps she had been wrong in thinking—during the weeks she had known him—that he was something of a stodge. Clearly there was more to Andrew Gordon than met the eye. Big, strong, silent men often had hidden depths.

They drove back to Crogers, and she waited outside while he made his offer. She felt it was tactful not to stick close and listen to every word. When he came out he looked even more excited; his fair-skinned face was flushed. 'He's getting in touch with the vendor. Of course, they don't like coming down, but I think there's a chance. . .at least he didn't laugh me out of court. Now, what do you say—' he turned to Kit in the confines of the little car, '—to a coffee at the Creamery? It's a favourite of the Dartings pupils; I've been there once or twice.'

So had Kit, on countless occasions, but she didn't mention this. 'I'd love it,' she said promptly, and as they left the car on the park behind the Regal Cinema she reflected that this was proving to be an enjoyable Saturday morning. It was with a light step that she preceded Andrew through the open doors of the Creamery restaurant some five minutes later, then jerked to a halt as she caught sight of Richard and Josie and the twins at one of the window-tables. Oh, no, she thought. No. . .not here. . .not now! Oh, why did Richard have to be with them? Why couldn't he be prodding someone in his surgery, not sitting here eating ice-cream.

'There's not a seat in sight; do you want to wait?' Andrew scanned the crowded room. He plainly hadn't spotted Josie, or hadn't recognised her back and he'd never met Richard. Quickly Kit pulled at his arm.

'Don't let's wait,' she said, at the same moment that Richard, looking up from speaking to one of the children, saw her standing there. He did a kind of double take at first, as though startled, or unsure, then he spoke to Josie, who swivelled round, and the two of them got up. They made beckoning signs. 'It's Josie and Richard; we'll have to go over.' Kit stepped forwards into the sea of closely set tables, followed by a less than willing Andrew, who would rather have gone further down the street to the Brass Lantern. He hated crowded rooms.

Richard, when they reached the window-table, was moving the twins along. 'They can sit on the window-seat, then you can have their chairs. How's that for good management?' Josie exclaimed, all smiles.

'Spot on!' Kit kissed the twins over tall ice-creams, then introduced Andrew to Richard, watching them shake hands. As she did so she couldn't help noticing how different the two men were—Richard lean and long, in a spanking white shirt, dark trousers and colourful tie, Andrew heavier, more casually dressed, more sparing with his smile. He ordered coffee for himself, and a vanilla ice for Kit, securing the quick service of a young waitress who had seen him before with pupils from the 'posh' school.

'*We've* got blinkerbottom glories,' Harry dug his spoon in deep.

'*Knicker*bocker glories, silly!' Daniel said crushingly.

'Knickers is rude; Mummy said so!'

'Not when it's ice-cream!'

This small argument had the grown-ups laughing, and the initial awkwardness of meeting unexpectedly began to take itself off.

'But what are you two doing in Melbridge?' Josie asked. 'Can't you keep away from the place? Andrew teaches history at the Dartings, darling.' She reached over and touched Richard's hand.

'You told me that, Jo, just before Kit moved.' He looked across at Andrew. 'So how are you liking living and working here in the Home Counties?' He leaned slightly forwards, making the hard wheelback chair creak. Kit was aware of his every movement, so aware that she felt she would burst. He was so close that she could see the grain of his skin, smell the cotton of his shirt. His attraction was potent; it overwhelmed her. Oh, think of something else. . .or someone else, she thought wildly, fastening her gaze on Andrew, who was saying that he liked the south of England and would probably make it his home.

'I've decided to buy a property in Melbridge; that's why we're here this morning. I can't live with Mrs Greenham in the long-term; it would hardly be fair, and was never my intention.' He tipped more cream into his cup. 'I've seen one property that I like very much, and have made an offer for it. It's actually in your road, Mrs Brett—a villa-type semi-detached that would divide very easily into two, and I could let the top half off.'

'Oh, I see. . .oh, yes, what a good idea!' Josie enthused. 'And I'm Josie, by the way. Not many people call me Mrs Brett these days.'

'All right, then, Josie,' he amended, flushing brick-red, which seemed to amuse her, and paved the way for teasing at which Josie was adept.

'So,' she went on, her eyes gleaming with mischief, 'if Kit gets fed up with living at home, and who wouldn't, for heaven's sake, she could move in with you. What could be cosier, or more convenient?'

She was mickey-taking, as Kit knew well, which wouldn't have mattered if the butt hadn't been Andrew, who wasn't the type to know how to turn the tables on her. She really was too bad. Kit was just about to say loudly and clearly that she liked living at home, when Andrew took the wind out of her sails, and Josie's too, by saying in all seriousness, 'Nothing would please me more, Josie. As a matter of fact I was going to suggest it to Kit—that is, if I get the house. It's ideally placed for both of us.' He caught Kit's eye and smiled.

He was calling Josie's bluff. He had to be; Kit felt pretty sure of that. Even so, for various reasons, she decided to play along.

'Wait and see if you get it first.' She returned his smile, allying with him, noticing, as she did so, that Josie's face was a study. She couldn't see Richard's; he was turned from her, dealing with Daniel, who was bent on turning his ice-cream glass upside-down on his head.

'Tell me more.' Josie looked arch, but any reply from either Kit or Andrew was hijacked by Richard, who made the point that they ought to be going, as they were having an early lunch. 'The last thing I feel like is eating.' Josie started to reach for the shopping-bags scattered round her chair. Richard helped her pick them up.

'Why the aversion to food?' Kit enquired, feeling thankful they were going.

'Oh, I've picked up some sort of bug, I think—keep going hot and cold. Would you believe it, in this hot weather! Come on, kids, scuttle,' she ordered, and Andrew got up to let the boys pass.

'We're going upriver on a boat to Hampton Court this afternoon', Daniel informed Kit, squeezing by, and giving her a hug.

'What a treat!' She returned his hug, resting her chin on the smooth crown of his head for a second. She had missed the twins so much.

'It's *down*river to Hampton Court from here,' Andrew put in. He wasn't a schoolmaster for nothing.

'Quite right,' Richard agreed, but there was the hint

of a smile in his voice. Hearing it, and catching his glance at Josie, Kit felt herself rear up. Andrew could no more help correcting a child's error than Richard could help, or resist, correcting a faulty diet that was making a patient ill. It was rude of him to be amused—rude and superior—so she glared at him, and got back in return a stony, grey-eyed stare.

When it boils down to it, she thought, watching him and Josie, flanked by the twins, making their way to the street outside, it doesn't take very much for us to be at loggerheads. Perhaps love, like beauty, is only skin-deep after all. For my sake I hope it is.

Two ladies in bowls hats came to take the two vacant chairs at the table. Their talk was all of the important away match to be played that afternoon. The heat and noise level in the overcrowded room was oppressing both of them.

In the car going home Andrew raised the subject of his house purchase again. 'I may hear something over the weekend,' he said. 'Croger promised to contact the vendor by phone and let me know at once.'

'It's a big step,' Kit ventured.

'But one that I've taken before.' Andrew stopped at a zebra crossing to let a tide of pedestrians flow past. 'I was on the verge of marrying, as I told you, and I bought a house at that time.'

'Oh, did you. . .? Oh, Andrew, I didn't realise!' She was anxious not to say the wrong thing.

'Contracts had been exchanged, so the thing was squarely in my lap. However——' he gave a tight smile '—I resold and made on the deal. And incidentally, Kit, I meant what I said in the café just now. If I get the Russell Road house there's nothing I'd like better than to offer you the tenancy of the top half—that is, if you want to move.'

Amazement that he hadn't been joking momentarily robbed Kit of speech. She knew, however, that she couldn't take him up on his offer—not because she didn't like him—she did—but because she felt it wouldn't work. Andrew was a fusser; he would probably object to all kinds of noises—like, for instance, her radio and television, which would be going on over his head. They would have to share a kitchen and bathroom, and she couldn't see that working either. She liked to eat when she felt like it, and do her washing as and when she could. There was absolutely no doubt about it—she would drive him mad in a week.

'It's good of you, Andrew—a fantastic offer—but I don't want to move,' she said. 'I've only just returned home, you see, after several years away. I know I shared with Jo for a time, but I'd rather be where I am, and there's another thing too that perhaps you've not thought of—the powers that be at the Dartings school might frown on one of their teachers setting what *they* might consider to be a bad example to the boys. I know I'd be there as a tenant only, but they might not see it that way.'

'This is the 1990s,' he laughed, but she could see that she'd struck the right note. He didn't look displeased or put down—merely a little surprised.

'You know,' she went on, trying to smooth the way even more, 'I quite thought you were joking—back in the café, I mean. I thought you were trying to "best" Josie, beat her at her own game.'

'I'm not much of a joker, as you probably realise. What I say I usually mean. It saves time and misunderstandings.' And with that he stretched out an arm and switched on the dashboard radio, releasing the soaring voice of Pavarotti, whose magic sound effectively stilled all commonplace noises like conversation for the rest of the journey home.

Once there, however, with the shopping unloaded, Andrew was off again, out to lunch with a teacher colleague and his family at Crayton. Mrs Greenham and Kit ate tongue and salad and *fromage frais* in the garden, then lay on loungers under the trees, with nothing more to disturb them than the hum of a power mower three doors up, and Daisy's heavy breathing as she lay in the grass with her head on Kit's sandalled foot. So peaceful was it that perhaps they should have known it couldn't last. Perhaps they should have recognised it for the lull before the storm.

The telephone rang the first time just before four o'clock, reverberating through the outside bell, startling Daisy into barks. Going in to answer it, Kit found herself speaking to Frank Croger, the estate agent, who asked for Mr Andrew Gordon in a deep, sepulchral voice. Andrew had asked her to take any message, and this she did, jotting down on the pad that his offer for the Russell Road house had been accepted. 'I'll tell him,' she promised, feeling excited on Andrew's behalf.

'And ask him to ring me on Monday, please,' Mr Croger intoned. Kit promised she would, then went back outside to tell her mother the news.

Mrs Greenham pushed her sunglasses down to the end of her nose. 'Well, I'm glad for his sake,' she said, 'but, selfishly, I can't help wishing he wasn't going quite so soon.'

'Oh, he'll probably be here for ages, Mummy. . .by

the time everything's through, and he's got the house furnished. It'll be two months at least.' Kit turned Daisy off her lounger and got back on to it.

'And you're still here—for the moment, anyway.' Mrs Greenham followed her daughter's example, and closed her eyes again.

Kit couldn't help wondering a little later, when she went in to fetch the tea, what her mother would have said if she'd accepted Andrew's offer and gone to live in his house. She would have assumed that 'there was something in it', that marriage would result, for she longed—as did most mothers—for her daughter to settle down. Yet it wasn't, Kit sighed, as simple as that, for it often took a long time to find the man you wanted to spend the rest of your life beside. And even when you did he might not feel the same way about you. He might be marriage-shy—or engaged to someone else.

They had finished tea and were still in the garden when the phone rang again. 'I'll answer it,' Mrs Greenham said promptly, setting aside the tray. She went off into the house at the double; she was one of those people who always expected whoever was calling to ring off at once.

Kit watched her go, watched her red and white skirt flash round the side of the porch then reappear so quickly that she couldn't believe she had answered the call. 'Kit. . . Kit!' she came running down the steps. 'Kit, that was Richard Anstey. Josie's ill. She's got to go into hospital; they're waiting for the ambulance now. He's going with her, and wants to know if you'll stay with the twins.'

'Ill. . . Josie!' Kit leapt up. 'But what. . .?'

'He said chest pains.'

'Oh, no. . .oh, God!' She grabbed her skirt, zipped it over her shorts, then sprinted across the lawn to the garage. 'Can you fetch my keys. . .? I think they're in my bedroom, on top of my bag!' She swung the garage door up. Within seconds Mrs Greenham reappeared with the keys.

'Bring the twins back here!' she shouted, running alongside the car.

It being five-thirty on a Saturday, the town was choked with traffic. In no way could Kit hurry; every set of lights seemed hell-bent on glowing red at her just as she approached. Surely it had never taken so long to get out to Melbridge? Impatience and fear notched up inside her. What was happening to Jo?

But at last she was there, passing the health centre, passing the church, making the turn that brought her straight into Russell Road. The ambulance was at the house, its doors standing wide. Josie was being brought out on a stretcher, Richard following. Graham Foxley, who was Josie's doctor, was standing at the front door. It took less than a minute to brake and get out and meet the stretcher at the ambulance doors. Seeing her, Josie grabbed her hand and held on for dear life. 'You're going to be all right, Jo.' Kit got in the ambulance with her, scarcely aware of doing so. 'Mum and I will look after the boys.'

'Take. . .them. . .home with you. . .'

'Yes, yes, of course.'

'Don't want. . .' Josie gasped for breath '. . .don't want them going away.'

'They won't be going anywhere, love, except home with me.'

An oxygen mask was being fitted over Josie's nose

and mouth; her eyes were eloquent above it. Kit squeezed her hand and got out, making way for Richard, whose face was as white as Josie's was cyanosed. 'Thanks, Kit, thanks for coming,' he said, just before the doors were closed.

The ambulance drew swiftly away, and Kit went into the house, where she found Dr Foxley blowing his nose in the hall. He suited his name; his features were sharp, while his hair was a blaze of red. 'Oh, Nurse Greenham.' He walked towards her. 'My wife is upstairs with the boys. When Richard rang me, I guessed she might be useful here.'

'That's kind of you, and of your wife.' Kit knew that the Foxleys and the Ansteys were friendly, which helped in times like these. 'I'm taking the children home with me,' she added. 'That's what Josie wants. My mother is only too willing to look after them, and so am I, of course.'

'Hoped you'd say that.' He tapped Kit's shoulder, and, encouraged by his smile—pointed to match his features—she asked what was wrong with Josie. He was cagey at first; doctors had that tendency, in case they might be wrong. 'Well, she has,' he admitted, 'an acute chest infection, that's all I can say at this stage. It's probably staphylococcal in origin, not uncommon at this time of year.'

'So, not a heart attack?' Kit moistened dry lips.

'No, not a heart attack.' He shook his head as he said this, but she wasn't reassured. Chest infection might mean severe lung infection, which might mean pneumonia of the staph. kind, which could carry in its train serious complications, sometimes fatal ones. Her mouth drained dry again.

The boys came pelting down the stairs, or rather, Daniel did. Harry was slower, one hand up high, trailing the banisters. 'Richard said you'd come; he said you'd look after us!' Daniel flung himself into Kit's arms. 'Mummy was sick and she kept coughing! Is she going to die?'

'Of *course* not.' Kit drew him off the stairs, so that Mrs Foxley could get by. 'Of course she's not going to die; she's just got ill like people do sometimes, even Harry and you. She's gone to hospital to be made well again, and you're both coming home with me to stay with Aunt Green just for a little while.'

Aunt Green was their name for Mrs Greenham, of whom they were both fond. 'She's looking forward to having you,' Kit added. 'Now let's go upstairs and pack your clothes, shall we, and one or two of your toys?'

'Will it be like a holiday?' Daniel's face brightened. Harry leaned against Kit's arm.

'A little like a holiday, perhaps, although you'll have to go to school.' Thanking Mrs Foxley for her help, Kit followed the boys upstairs.

All the time they were deciding on what to pack, she kept her worst fears hidden, for anxiety had a way of conveying itself, and a child could latch on fast. She thought she had put on a pretty good act, for when they were leaving the house Daniel skipped happily down the path to where she'd left the car. Not so Harry, however; he waited for Kit, sticking so close when she locked the front door that she could scarcely move her legs. 'Kit, are you sure Mummy won't die?' he asked in a wobbly voice.

'I'm quite sure.' She bent down to him, not daring, even then, to look him in the face for long, in case he should read in her eyes any trace of his own question. . .was his mother going to die?

CHAPTER SIX

IT WAS nine p.m. and the twins were in bed when Richard's car drew up at Ford House and he swung his legs stiffly out. Kit heard the door slam and ran out to meet him; she was desperate for news. 'I rang the hospital twice, but they didn't say much!' She all but dragged him into the house, where he told her and her mother that Josie was in Intensive Care.

'She's got staph. pneumonia,' he said flatly, sinking down into a chair.

'But how quick. . . Kit said you all met this morning!' Mrs Greenham was the first to speak.

'That strain of pneumonia *is* sudden; it can literally strike like a knife. All the same—' he looked pensive '—she must have been showing *some* signs earlier on—during the morning, I mean. I just didn't notice them.'

'Well, don't blame yourself for that,' Kit said stoutly. 'I didn't notice she looked unwell—in the café, I mean—not until she admitted to going hot and cold. Jo can put a pretty good face on things—often does, for the sake of the twins.'

'She was never what you would call robust, not even as a child,' Mrs Greenham said, as she went out of the room to make some sandwiches.

'She's very ill, isn't she?' Kit whispered before she came back.

'At the moment, yes.' Richard's eyes met hers; he knew she couldn't be fooled.

'She'll have every care, though.'

'Well, of course she will; the County's a fine hospital.'

Their conversation was forced and spasmodic. Richard looked tired to death, but at least, Kit thought, he *came* here, he didn't just telephone. His head was bent; he was fondling Daisy, who was sniffing round his shoes. It was still light outside, and the room was orange-streaked by the dying sun. The patio doors were half open and the scents of the garden drifted in, but brought no comfort, only added an extra poignancy. . . an extra sadness, laced with fear, to the scene.

Mrs Greenham came back with the sandwiches, which they all tried to eat. There was coffee too, good and strong, which went down more easily. 'Let's hope that we have good news tomorrow,' she said prosaically. Even she knew it wasn't the most original of remarks, but at least it got her white-faced daughter and the young doctor out of their trance.

'She's having the best of care, Mrs Greenham—' Richard made an effort '—and it's put her mind at rest knowing that Harry and Daniel are here. She didn't want them going down to Sussex, out of her reach.'

'My dear Richard.' Mrs Greenham threw formality to the winds. 'My dear boy, I shall love having them. I've got the room and I've got the time. I can take them to school, take them to see their mother later on. I expect that's what Josie had in mind; she didn't want them far away.'

'Even so,' Richard said thoughtfully, as he refilled his cup, 'even so, the Telfords, her parents, will have to be told. I had to give Sister their number. She'll contact them tonight. In this kind of situation it's the usual thing.'

'Oh, poor dears!' Mrs Greenham sighed.

'They're bound to come.' Kit's throat tightened, her anxiety taking fresh hold. She shivered and clutched the arms of her chair. Richard saw her knuckles gleam white.

'The antibiotics, once they get a grip, should work wonders, Kit.' He leaned towards her, smiling, masking his own deep fears. She was doing the same for his sake, yet each of them knew the score.

In her chair by the window Mrs Greenham's thoughts were with her friends, the Telfords. She put herself in their place. Whatever would she do if Kit fell ill and was fighting to survive? The sound of the front door opening and closing brought her to her feet. 'That will be Andrew,' she muttered, going out into the hall. Kit and Richard could hear her telling him that the twins were upstairs, and why. . .'So if you don't mind being quiet, dear. . .not that you're ever anything else. Oh, and your offer for the house has been accepted; Kit took the message. She'll want to tell you about it.'

'I must be on my way,' Richard said, his voice blotting out Andrew Gordon's reply to Mrs Greenham's news.

The two men met in the hall—Andrew looking a little confused. 'I'm so sorry about your fiancée. . . It must have been very sudden.' His eyes wandered to Kit, so perhaps the house news was uppermost in his mind.

'Yes, it was sudden,' Richard was saying, shaking his head at Mrs Greenham's invitation to peep at the twins. 'I'll come and see them tomorrow, Mrs Greenham—that is, if I may.'

'Of course, Richard, any time. . .any time at all.' She

opened the door for him, leaving it ajar for Kit to come back in, for she was going out to the car.

Josie's condition worsened over the next three days—the complication of empyema following pleurisy. She had a high fever with rigor, and knew neither Richard nor Kit, nor her parents, who were staying in the town.

Kit was hard put to it to know what to tell the twins, but she agreed with Richard and their grandparents that a white lie would be best. 'It may take longer than we thought,' she explained, 'to get Mummy well, so you can't visit her just yet, because she gets very tired.'

Richard went to Grantford to see them whenever he could and, worried though he was, he never showed it with them. With Kit he could let down his guard; he could talk about his worst fears. Pretence that everything would be all right had long since been abandoned, for they both knew that Josie had less than an even chance of survival.

On Tuesday, as an emergency measure, she was taken down to theatre, where a rib resection was performed and the empyema drained off. 'She's desperately weak,' Richard said when he went over to Ford House that evening. Kit was in the garden spraying roses, rubber gloves and sunglasses protecting her hands and eyes. Mrs Greenham had told him he would find her there; he had already said goodnight to the twins, and told Mrs Greenham how Josie was. Now he was telling Kit, who joined him on the patio, taking off her gloves and glasses and laying them down on the seat.

'She's bound to be weak after surgery, isn't she? But

having that fluid drained off *must* help her breathing.' Kit screwed up her eyes in the sun.

'They seem fairly pleased with her.' Richard's voice was low-pitched.

'Well, there you are'. Kit eased round to face him. 'Jo will fight this thing, you know. She's got so much to live for, and look forward to, and, although she always looks fragile, she's determined, and that kind of attitude wins battles, even when you're ill.'

'You're a good friend.' He was looking straight ahead down the long, bordered garden, to the little orchard at the end where Kit and her mother had lazed the afternoon away last Saturday, when Josie had been taken ill.

'I wish I could be a magic friend, able to wave a wand over Josie's bed and make her well. I wish I could rush in the house, up the stairs into the twins' bedroom, to tell them, with perfect truth, that their mother was well enough to see them, and couldn't wait to do so.'

'I wish it too.' He got up to go.

And I also wish, she thought to herself as she saw him off, that I could take that look of strain from his face; he looks like a haunted man. She went back to her spraying, mixing more fungicide, plunging her hands in her gloves. It had been, was still being a terrible week. Was it never going to end? Somehow or other, she was doing her job, and she knew that Richard was coping, but the struggle to ignore, even for an hour, the trauma of Josie was a hard business, like a terrible tug of war.

Kit went to see Josie during her lunch-break on Thursday, and it seemed as she sat there, tense and silent by her bed, that Josie had shrunk to half her size.

A drip ran into her right arm, and a drain ran out of her chest; she was propped up high to help breathing and drainage, and she appeared to be asleep. Kit sat there and thought about her, letting her mind slip back to memories of the two of them at five years old, meeting for the first time at school, almost too shy to speak. She thought of children's parties, of speech days and sports days, of their first teenage disco, of foursomes with boyfriends, of Josie meeting Paul, of the glamour and glitz of her wedding, of Josie's phone call a year after that to tell her the twins had been born.

You have got to get well, Jo, she breathed. *You have got to get well*, so come on, give it your best shot, you can make it if you try.

And perhaps, who knew, this feverish behest had a magic-wand effect. Perhaps something of its intensity reached the sick girl on the bed, for during that night there was a change in her condition, a slight change for the better. The improvement continued throughout Friday, and by teatime of that day she was less febrile; the antibiotics could be seen to be doing their work. She was lucid enough, strong enough to say a word or two, and the next day she was able to be transferred from Intensive Care into a side-room off one of the medical wards. One of the first things she wanted was to see her children, and Kit took them in on Sunday. They were awed by the hospital atmosphere, but thrilled to see their mother. Once again Josie made Kit promise to keep them at Grantford. 'I want them near me; I want to see them every single day.'

The Telfords motored back to Sussex on Sunday, for hotels didn't run themselves. As soon as Josie was strong enough she would go there to convalesce. She was told, however, that this was unlikely to be for another two or three weeks. 'Then in that case I can take the boys with me,' she said, 'for it'll be their school holidays.'

Richard was in seeing her every day, and he also, whenever he could, dropped in at Ford House to help Mrs Greenham and Kit with the twins. 'He's so good with those children,' Mrs Greenham said one evening when he had been. 'Josie's a very lucky girl to find a man like him.'

'I agree, she is.' Kit was through in her bedroom, changing her shoes. 'But she's not so lucky in other respects. Apparently her heart has been weakened by all that she's been through. She won't have to live the life of an invalid—nothing like that—but she will have to be careful, and not do silly things.'

'Oh, dear!' Mrs Greenham digested this. 'Does she know?' she asked.

'Yes, she knows. Jo's not a coward—she likes to know the facts—but she doesn't seem to be worrying about it. She more or less tossed it off—said she was born lazy, anyway, so now she'd have a good excuse.'

'What does Richard say?'

'Not a lot—at least, not to me—but I expect he and Josie have talked it through. Plenty of people have damaged hearts and live to a ripe old age.'

'He'll look after her, being a doctor,' Mrs Greenham emphasised, bringing wet towels out of the bathroom to dry.

'I'm sure he will.' Kit's back was to her mother, and she kept it so for a minute. If anything she loved Richard more since Josie's illness. He had turned to her during it, which endeared him to her more, made her

feel proud and glad to be around when he wanted her. Even so, how ironic it was that, having moved from Josie's house to avoid seeing so much of him, she was now meeting him in her own home, where she'd assumed he would never come.

During the following week she fell in with Andrew's wishes and went out with him most evenings. He called it 'escaping' and made no secret of it, either. 'I know it's your mother's house, Kit,' he said one evening, 'but I'm in the company of children all day at school, and the last thing I want is the noise and clamour of another pair when I get home at night.'

Kit sympathised because, to a certain extent, she could see his point of view. The twins, like most other little boys, were noisy and boisterous. They loved 'jumping' the stairs, making bomb-like landings, they liked shrieking in the bath, and they liked playing with Daisy, who, being young herself, added her barks to their din. Even Mrs Greenham sang songs when she cooked the supper. 'Dashing away with the Smoothing Iron' and 'Cock-a-Doodle-Do', not to mention 'Christopher Robin', were all part of her repertoire.

'I'm sorry, Andrew, I really am. I'll have a word with Mother, see if we can tone it down a bit. It can't be much fun for you.' There was a degree of tongue in the cheek about this remark of Kit's, but all the same she would—when Andrew was in—try to quieten the boys, then he wouldn't be obliged to mark piles of books after ten o'clock, poor man!

By the end of August, maybe even before then, he'd be living in his own house. The purchase seemed to be going through all right, so by the autumn term he would be installed, and have all the peace in the world.

And round about that time, Kit thought with a pang, she would be girding herself up for the ordeal of attending Richard's and Josie's wedding which—now that Josie was getting well—wouldn't have to be postponed indefinitely. I'll get through it all right, she told herself, and she didn't doubt that she would, but fairly soon afterwards—and she had made up her mind about this only recently—she was going to apply for another position right away from Surrey, probably in the Midlands again, or even further north. She couldn't act a part forever, could she? And to have to keep running into Richard and Josie as a married couple was something she couldn't face. Her mother, not knowing the true state of affairs, would be disappointed, of course; so, presumably, would her colleagues and the supervisor. But I can't help that, she reasoned stoically; only I know what's best.

All this passed through her mind one morning as she drove out to Crayton to see one of her antenatals—Eileen Purle—who was due to give birth any day. 'I can't wait to get it over,' she said, when Kit asked her how she was. 'It's due this weekend, but of course you know that,' she sighed dramatically, but with difficulty too, as even her chest felt overwhelmed with weight. 'I've told Colin to let you know when I go in. You'll come and see me, won't you?' She stared at Kit's smooth sun-browned arms as she took a blood-pressure reading. Kit Greenham was the prettiest of all the midwives, and the one whom Eileen liked best.

'I'll come and see you, and that's a promise.' Kit loosened the cuff of the blood-pressure-reading machine and put it back in her case. 'You've had no more cramps in your legs, I hope?'

'No, those seem to have gone. I suppose you could say I'm very well.' She went to the door with Kit, brushing aside the latter's instruction to stay where she was. 'Oh, I like to lumber around,' she laughed. 'I can't see my feet, but that doesn't mean I can't make use of them; they've got to do their job.' In spite of her laughter, Kit knew she was anxious, but at this stage of pregnancy, with her baby pitched and ready for birth, anxiety was natural.

What wasn't so natural, although it sometimes happened, was the attitude of one of her new mothers, Natalie Jeeves, whom she saw that afternoon. She didn't, she said, love her child; she just couldn't take to him. 'And he doesn't like me, either, or my husband. He's always crying, and he looks at us as though he doesn't want to be here. He wakes us up four or five times in the night; he just doesn't seem to fit in!'

She looked thin and pale, and exhausted, and Kit felt sorry for her, but even more sorry for baby Simon, who was yelling his head off, stiffening his tiny body, holding his arms out straight. 'Babies have no sense of timing, Natalie.' Kit took the child out of his cot. 'They don't realise that when it's night-time their parents want to sleep; they don't understand why they can't be feeding exactly when they want, as they did when they were inside their mother. . . Being born is a puzzle to them. That's why Simon is being antisocial. He thinks it's a rum old world.'

'Well, there's nothing I can do about *that*, is there?' Natalie looked truculent.

'Yes, there is.' Kit shifted the now quiet baby more comfortably in her arms. 'There are things you can do to make him happier, which will make him respond to you. He knows who you are; he knows you're his mother—babies instinctively know their mothers—so hold him more, cuddle him more, talk and sing to him. He's such a lovely baby, a handsome lad, so why not tell him so?'

'He won't understand.'

'He will, you know; he understands more than you think.'

Natalie's face was a study in doubt, but as she took her son from Kit she held him closer to her, up against her breast, with her arms tight around him, instead of lying him flat on her lap with his face turned up to the sky. Due to poor lactation, which wasn't her fault, she wasn't breast-feeding Simon. Even so, at just twelve days old, his birthweight had been regained. Kit took the trouble to congratulate her on this, for praise meant so much. 'You're doing so well. . .both of you. . . All you need is to get to know one another, and that's largely up to you.'

Natalie sighed audibly, 'I didn't think it would be like this. We purposely went in for a baby, and I thought that when he came I'd love him straight off. . .bingo! I didn't know I'd have to learn.'

'Bonding isn't always instant,' Kit told her gently. 'Sometimes mothers have to persevere to bring it about.'

'It isn't that I don't *want* to love him.'

'No, of course not; I understand that.'

The baby began to cry again, and Natalie's face contorted. 'When are you coming again?' she asked above the ensuing din.

'I'm off this weekend, but I'll be coming on Monday, or one of us will,' Kit promised, but decided, as she drove away from the house, to consult with Megan Lee, the health visitor, about Natalie Jeeves. Her depression, she felt sure, was temporary and would lift once the baby slept better at night. Even so, this might be a case when two heads were better than one.

She was nearly to the end of Riverside Lane when she caught sight of Jill Libbots pushing her baby, a fair-headed man strolling by her side. The man was in naval officer's uniform, so had to be Jill's husband. Kit had never met him before, but it was to see how the baby was that she decided to stop the car and have a word with them. Gemma, at eleven weeks old, was no longer on her list, so it was interesting to see how she had grown, and grown she had. . . There she lay under her sun canopy, a rounded, golden-limbed child, with blue eyes to match the sky, and bright hair just starting to grow.

'She's absolutely gorgeous.' Kit couldn't stop looking at her.

'And her eyes cleared up as you said they would.' Jill smiled down at her child.

'Thank you for the care you gave my wife.' Sub-lieutenant Libbots shook Kit's hand, as Jill introduced him, coming round to her side. He had bold eyes—blue like his daughter's—and they moved over Kit's face with slow deliberation, while his tightly clasping hand appeared to have no intention of relaxing its hold. A ladies' man, Kit thought amusedly, recalling the old saying about sailors having a girl in every port.

'Are you home on long leave?' she asked him, removing her hand.

'Ten days. I've only just come, and once I'm changed out of this. . .' a sweeping arm indicated his uniform,

'. . .I'll be settling down to fatherhood, and giving a hand with the chores.'

'I'm dragging him over to Grantford Fair on Saturday,' said Jill, tilting the pram so that Gemma could see Kit getting back into her car.

Where the world and his wife will meet, thought Kit, waving goodbye to the little family at the kerbside and driving towards the town.

The fair was to Grantford as the regatta was to Henley—an important annual event. It couldn't go back so far in years, but it could tot a good few up. It had been started between the wars, and had continued ever since, held on the first Saturday in July, whatever the weather brought. Kit hadn't been to it since she was seventeen—her last year at home—but before then she and Josie had gone every year. Josie had met Paul Brett there; he had been staying in the area, auditing the books of a local firm.

This year Kit was taking the twins, who were looking forward to it. Mrs Greenham was one of the principal stallholders, and had been preparing for weeks. All the takings—the gate-money and whatever the stallholders made—would be going to her favourite charity, the British Red Cross.

The Dartings School was having a woodwork stall—shelving, cabinets, stools and small tables, made by the pupils. Andrew, therefore, was keen to go, so it had better be a fine day, Kit thought, watching him press his trousers on Friday afternoon.

CHAPTER SEVEN

SATURDAY dawned not only fine, but sunny, cloudless and warm. If anything it was *too* warm, and Mrs Greenham was 'phewing' and shaking the neck of her dress as early as seven a.m.

Andrew, the picture of coolness, his fawn hair damp from the shower, offered to take her jams and marmalade, curd and home-made yoghurt down to the fairground in his car, and help her load up her stall. Kit, left at home with the children, gave them their breakfast, then hustled them into the Renault for a quick shopping trip, stocking up on the usual provisions for the weekend. It was ten-thirty by the time she and the boys set off for Challoners Field—the area of grassland behind the museum, where the fair was in full swing. They could hear it long before they got there, the music of the town band vying with that of the steam-driven roundabout pumping out old English airs like 'Strawberry Fair', and 'The Eton Boating Song'.

Kit caught some of the twins' excitement as they pushed through the turnstiles. There were crowds of people—waves of them—and still more were pouring in. Some wore fancy costumes; there was colour everywhere. Bunting dripped from the trees, balloons floated from stalls, and a castle trampoline wobbled about like an orange jelly next to the hoop-la stall. There was a Jack-and-Jill helter-skelter, and donkey rides for the under-sevens; there was a bran tub, an Aunt Sally, and a Punch and Judy show. But the *pièce de résistance* was the big, solid, ponderous roundabout, with its gleaming brass fitments, and its coloured animals whirling round and round. People were queuing up for rides—adults as well as children—a good deal of jostling went on; the noise level was high. Stewards with loudhailers were requesting that all litter be placed in the bins, and that people with dogs keep them restrained on leads. Near the refreshments marquee, on its own parking space, was an ambulance and crew. . .in case disaster strikes, thought Kit, relieved to see it there.

Pushing the twins in front of her, she made her way over to the Dartings' stall, where she and Andrew had arranged to meet, only to find that a minor disaster had already struck there. The senior boy who'd had charge of the stall had fainted in the heat, and Andrew had been asked to take over until the afternoon. 'I'm so sorry about it, Kit; it's a nuisance, I know. . .' he broke off to serve a young couple with a stool '. . but I'll have to stay here until a replacement can be found.'

'Don't worry about it,' Kit assured him—quite needlessly, she felt, for Andrew was plainly enjoying himself, looking every inch the young schoolmaster, filling in the breach. He hadn't really wanted to tag round the fair with the children, she knew, and after lunch he wouldn't have to, for Richard was picking them up and taking them to the hospital to see their mother, and out to tea afterwards.

'I like your dress; it suits you.' He managed to get that in, leaning over a bookcase to do so, before she took her leave.

Kit's dress was a drop-waisted cream cotton, calf-length and cool. It showed off her lightly tanned arms and legs, made her brown eyes look even more dark, and was a perfect foil for her hair, which gleamed as gold as the sun itself. Male heads turned her way as, with the twins pushing in front, she fought through to the trampoline, where she paid for the boys to bounce up and down in shrieking delight for the next fifteen minutes or so.

While standing there, she collected news and saw several people she knew. A nurse from the hospital told her that Eileen Purle had given birth to a son at midnight, weighing all of eight pounds. Jill Libbots and her husband passed by and stopped to have a word. Mark Libbots was in jeans and T-shirt, carrying his baby daughter—winsome under her sun-bonnet—as though she was precious cargo, which it was obvious she was. Lucky devils, Kit thought, watching them move on. He may be flirty, but it's harmless enough. He plainly adores Jill *and* his daughter; they're a happy family, and that's what counts in the end.

A few minutes later she saw another mother from Crayton village—Rose Garner, who was helping with the donkeys. Daniel and Harry wanted a ride. 'I've got a job at the sanctuary,' Rose grinned. 'Full-time, too. I can take Tom with me all day—Miss Cartwright doesn't mind.' She pointed forwards along the track where the twins were in the saddle. 'That's her, with your two boys. She looks a funny old thing, but she's all right; so's her sister. I'm really enjoying the job.'

'I expect they're glad of the help, Rose. Now, tell me, how's Tom getting on?'

'Oh, smashing. Mum's got him today—well, till teatime, anyway.'

Kit stood chatting to her until the boys had finished

their ride, when she had to tell them, very firmly, for they wanted to stay on, that they must go and see Aunt Green on her stall, or she'd be very hurt and upset.

'We want to go on the roundabout.' Daniel rubbed the seat of his shorts. Once off the donkey he could feel its effects; the saddle had been very hard.

'You can go on everything when we've seen Aunt Green.'

'Can we have an ice-cream?'

'Yes, that too.'

'And some candy-floss?'

Kit sighed and said, 'Yes,' again. Did all small boys want everything in sight, and all at once, as well?

They reached Mrs Greenham's stall at last, and saw her standing there, flushed under her tall chef's hat, handing out her wares, taking money and giving change with brisk efficiency. 'I'm doing wonderfully well, dear,' she called out when she saw Kit. 'I wish I'd made twice as much marmalade; that's very popular. Now, hang on, don't go away.' She served two more customers, then said quickly, for she couldn't waste time, 'Richard is here; he got rid of his patient—well, you know what I mean. He's over by the bookstall; I said I would tell you. How's Andrew getting on?'

'Fine,' was all Kit had time to say, before her mother had swung round to serve an old man with apricot preserve.

The bookstall was near the roundabout, and there, among weaving arms reaching out for musty volumes and dog-eared paperbacks, was Richard with his jacket slung over one shoulder, looking out over the crowd. He spotted Kit in her cream dress, the two little boys at her side. He went forward to meet them, then the boys were upon him, excitedly calling his name.

'Hi, there, what a scrum!' His eyes smiled into Kit's.

'You can say that again!' She looked down at the boys, suddenly shy of him.

'I've been along to the Dartings' stall. . .heard what had happened. . .tough on Gordon.'

'Oh, I don't know,' Kit said. 'He'll be free after lunch, and it's tougher on the pupil who fainted, I should think.' She didn't intend to sound quite so dismissive, 'Well, you know what I mean,' she added quickly, trying to make amends.

'Yes, I know what you mean.' The crowd had pushed them closer together. Behind their heads the roundabout was starting up again. Horses and weird-looking creatures like cockerels began to revolve, slowly at first, then faster and faster, to the deafening sound of music from the fifties, beginning with 'Blueberry Hill'.

'Can we go on next time. . .*can* we?' Daniel appealed to Richard, who, glancing at Kit and seeing her nod, told the twins they could.

'It means queuing, though; you can't just walk on. See, look there.' He pointed to the line of children and parents stretching back very nearly to Mrs Greenham's stall.

'Why can't we stay here and get on quickly when the music stops? There won't be room for everyone.' Daniel's glance at the long queue was one of dismay. . . Why, it might take *years* to get on.

'You can't jump the queue. You must wait your turn; that's the way it goes. So, come on, now.' Richard reached for his hand. 'Let's get to the end. Kit and I will wait with you and pay the man when the time comes.'

'I don't suppose it will take *too* long, Danny.' Harry always tried to console his brother when he pulled a long, miserable face.

'I bet it will, though,' Richard whispered against Kit's ear. 'They'll never get this lot on in one go. We're about two rides behind.'

'In that case, wait for squalls,' Kit said equally softly. 'What it is to be *in loco parentis*.'

'Especially at a fair!' They were holding hands, but only, Kit told herself, to keep altogether. She turned her attention to the roundabout. It was going more slowly now. . .more and more slowly. . . Now it had stopped, and so had the music.

'It's stopped, it's stopped; they're getting off! Will it be our turn now? Kit, will it be our turn?' Harry stepped back on Kit's foot. The queue began to move forward. . .would they get on? They were nearly to the platform, nearly to the steps. It really looked as though they might just make it, might just squeeze on—that was, if they shared a horse.

'No more after the boys in blue!' shouted the man in charge. This was fine, for the 'boys in blue' were the twins; it was going to be all right. But then, just as they were six from the platform, just as Richard was feeling in his pocket for the fare, two girls aged about nine or ten squeezed in front of Daniel, pushing him and Harry backwards. . .when pandemonium broke out.

'That's not fair. . .that's not fair!' Daniel's shout was almost a scream. Seizing the dress of the nearest girl, he spun her sideways out of the queue. She turned round and hit him. Harry sprang to his defence, the other girl hit Harry, and in seconds flat the four of them were kicking and punching and rolling on the grass. The queue skirted them, and moved on; the roundabout started up. Richard and Kit separated the fighters. Daniel had a bleeding nose. Harry, red with fury, was on the point of tears, while the two girls were defended by their mother, who called the boys hooligans.

'They were provoked; they had been standing in the queue for the last five minutes,' Richard said, raising his voice against the blare of the roundabout music.

'I didn't know that,' the woman mouthed.

'You probably didn't see.'

'No, I didn't.' She was grateful for the loophole, so much so that she made her daughters say sorry, before she quickly led them away.

'She might have asked if the boys were all right.' Kit was mopping up Daniel's nose, which had bled freely down his front and hers, making a mess of her dress.

'Boys should never hit girls,' Richard told them, but was gentle in doing so. 'And now, what do we do with you both?' But this was soon solved by Mrs Greenham appearing at Kit's elbow. She had seen the whole thing from her stall.

'What rough little girls. . .badly brought up! Come here, sweetheart, let me look.' She drew Daniel to her, reassuring him and giving him little pats. 'Noses bleed very easily; there's nothing to be frightened of. Still, we must change your shirt, mustn't we? There's a lady over there selling some, so we can buy you one and slip it on behind my stall.' She looked at Kit, at the vivid stain on the bodice of her dress. 'Dear me, you'll have to go home and get into something else! You look as though someone's knifed you!'

'Over my dead body,' Richard whispered softly for Kit's ears alone.

'Take my car, dear, and go now.' Mrs Greenham dabbed cautiously at Daniel's nose, kneeling down on the grass.

'Oh, I'll drive her, Mrs Greenham.' Richard slid Harry down from his back.

'And I'll keep the children here with me.' Mrs Greenham gathered them up. 'Once they're over the shock of doing battle we'll go on the roundabout.'

'*Will* we?' The twins perked up.

'Of course, why not? It's a long time since Aunt Green had a ride on a roundabout.'

'What about your stall?' Kit tried to cover the gory stain with her hand.

'I've a helper; she's there now, taking over until after lunch. Now, come along, boys; we mustn't waste time. We'll see you back——' she beamed over at Kit and Richard '—at the entrance to the luncheon marquee soon after half-past twelve.'

'Your mother rises to the occasion, doesn't she?' Richard remarked as they drove the short distance to Ford House, avoiding the High Street with its build-up of traffic still coming through to the fair.

'She's always been like that—very resourceful. And she's not a clinging type—a bit bossy, but unclinging.' Kit relaxed in the passenger seat.

'Has she been a widow long?' he asked.

'Nearly eleven years, since I was fifteen. Dad died of influenzal pneumonia in the February of that year. He was a publisher and worked in town. Mother always swears he caught the bug travelling up and down.'

'More than likely.'

'It was so quick too, you know, which made it such a shock.' Kit hesitated fractionally, then decided to go on. 'I think that's why I was so scared when Josie fell ill. Her infection wasn't due to flu, but there was the same rapid onset. And, talking of Josie, isn't it fantastic that she's recovering so well? When you think that only a fortnight ago—a fortnight ago today——'

'I was sending for Graham Foxley,' Richard interrupted, 'cursing myself for not having noticed she was sickening for something serious several hours before.'

'You can't always tell.'

'I'm a doctor, Kit!'

'Even so, you can't always tell.'

'I'd upset her that morning; we'd had an argument. I was blind to everything else.' He seemed determined to censure himself, and this made her cross, as well as curious about their argument. What had it been about?

'I'm sure Jo won't hold that against you. She can be difficult, I know, like most women!' She flicked a glance at him, intending him to laugh. He didn't, though; he looked grim-faced, and his mouth was a tight line.

Conscious of having said too much, or completely the wrong thing, she stared out of the nearside window, fighting a bleakness that the brilliance of the morning and the warmth of the sun did nothing to dispel.

When they reached Ford House Richard turned the car ready for driving back. 'Don't forget to first-aid your dress,' he said, as they crossed the lawn.

'Daniel certainly spread himself.' Kit looked down at herself. 'It could have been quite nasty, Richard, if you hadn't stopped that fight. The girls were a good deal older and heavier than the twins.'

'It amazed me how Harry waded in.'

'He would; he always supports Daniel, even though he's the quieter child.'

'You love those kids, don't you?'

'I admit it.' She gave a shrug.

'Lucky little boys!'

'Yes, aren't they?' She laughed, but her heart began to beat fast.

The house had that empty, no-one-there feeling, as they let themselves into the hall. The sun streaming through the landing window sent a shaft of light down the stairs. Dust *motes* danced through it; somewhere near at hand an insect was zinging against a window-pane. Apart from that the silence was absolute, or it seemed so to Kit, who was aware of nothing and no one but Richard standing close behind her back. He was so close that when she slid her shoulder-bag down to the floor her hand knocked against his front and she heard his indrawn breath.

'Sorry!'

'It's all right.'

Their voices cut the silence; she began to move to the stairs.

'Where's Daisy?' He sounded a long way behind her.

'Left with the people next door.'

'Of course. . .yes.'

Talking trivia helped. She began to mount the stairs. . .up, and up, and up. . .and with each step she took the distance between her and the man she loved lengthened and tension eased, the silence of the house losing its power to excite with promises.

Once on the landing, caught in the dazzle of light from the window, it was safe to turn round and call out, 'Why don't you go through and sit out on the patio? You'll find it much cooler there.'

'I'll do that, thanks.' His voice sounded muffled. He moved off down the passage, and, as Kit stood in the bathroom, stripping off her dress, she could hear him springing the bolt on the doors, hear him sliding them back and stepping outside, when immediately she felt not relieved but bereft.

Through in her bedroom, opening her cupboard, she took out a pair of white jeans, stepped into them, and zipped them up, smoothing them over her hips. A yellow and white striped top came next, and a white Alice band held back her hair from her face, which still wore a strained expression. She told herself to buck up. . . The world isn't well lost for love; there's too much else going on.

Her dressing-table was set in the window, and as she raised the net curtain she saw that Richard had moved to the bottom of the garden, and was walking among the trees. His hands were plunged into his pockets, his dark head was bent, and he was pacing rather than merely walking, the overhead sun shortening his shadow, pooling it round his feet.

Kit sighed. She attracted him strongly; she couldn't help knowing that. She also knew that it bothered him; he had a conscience, like her. He was loyal to Josie, whom he adored. Dalliance wasn't his style, but then neither was it hers. And she too loved Josie, which was why—as soon as she could—she was going to move right out of the district, which would solve the problem for good.

Moving the curtain back into place, she ran downstairs and out into the garden, waving and calling to him. He waved back, and she went to meet him, not hurrying at all; she was walking really quite slowly, but the spring in her step was apparent and her eyes shone. . . How blissful it was to be walking towards him, instead of moving away.

'You look like a slender, elegant boy,' he told her when they met, catching hold of her hands and swinging them. 'Except, of course, that you're just about the most feminine creature I've ever come across.'

'What a pretty speech!' She bobbed a curtsy. She felt frivolous and light.

'I'm famous for them!' He caught her mood, raising her hands and holding them against his chest, smiling into her eyes. She could feel his heart beating, feel his warmth, feel her hands yearning to move up and round his neck. It didn't take very much to change a mood from light to heavy. . .from frivolous to serious. . . from safe to dangerous. She pulled her hands free and talked about getting back.

'The first lunch-sitting is at half-twelve. Mother and the boys will be waiting for us, champing at the bit.'

'That I don't doubt,' he agreed at once, and they walked back to the car, which felt like an oven inside and smelled of leather seats. 'You could fry eggs in here!' he said irritably, spinning the windows down.

'It'll be all right once we get going.' Kit shot a glance at him. He stretched out an arm to switch on the engine, but said nothing more until they were out on the road, when, thrusting on his glasses, he asked her what she was going to do that afternoon.

'Do the rounds of the fair, sample everything, help

Mother pack up her stall, then go home and change,' she replied.

'For a party?'

'No, for afternoon tea at the Dartings School. I met the head and his wife in Melbridge last week. Andrew introduced me, and the invite followed on.'

'Are you interested?' The question was casually put, yet even she sensed its loaded quality.

'I'm interested in the school. I'm also interested in Andrew as a *friend*. There's nothing wrong with that, I hope!'

'Absolutely not.' He pursed his lips then straightened them. 'Except, of course, that the psychologists would have us believe that platonicism between the sexes is something of a myth.'

'Yes, I've heard that, and I've proved it to be wrong. . .well, once or twice, anyway!' She laughed, which made him do so as well, and the atmosphere eased. 'So, could you tell Josie,' she went on, 'that I may be a little late getting to the hospital tonight? I don't want her worrying, or anything like that.'

'Of course I'll tell her,' he said easily, his eyes on the car in front. 'She's improving quite dramatically now; that course of physio is doing wonders for her breathing. She looks a different girl. Even so, we've got to postpone the wedding for a few weeks.'

'Yes, she told me that. There's no point in rushing things.'

He acknowledged this with a nod, and Kit dragged her eyes from his face with an effort, and looked out of the window.

They were nearly back to the fairground, and as they turned left by the museum there it was in front of them, spinning with colour and din. Being a doctor Richard was allowed to leave his car on the grass by the ambulance. 'No alarms or excursions, I hope?' he asked one of the crew, as he and Kit got out in the blinding sunshine again.

'No, it's what you might call a rest-cure, sir,' the girl attendant said. 'I'm beginning to wish I'd brought my bikini!' She nudged Kit and winked. '*Some* people have all the luck!' She was drooling at Richard's back.

But he's on loan only, Kit thought sadly, catching him up and walking with him to the big-top marquee, where they met the twins and her mother for lunch.

CHAPTER EIGHT

'I HEAR they did well at the fair on Saturday,' Megan Lee, the health visitor, remarked to Kit on Tuesday when they met soon after lunch. They were in Richard's surgery, as he and Kit were to share the clinic, seeing women with special problems affecting their pregnancies. Richard hadn't yet arrived, and Megan, seeing Kit there, had dropped in to have a chat before she set off on her calls.

'They did wonderfully well,' Kit agreed. 'My mother took over a hundred pounds on her stall—not bad for home-made jams.'

'I caught sight of you once.' Megan perched on the corner of Richard's desk. 'You were queuing up for the roundabout with Josephine Brett's little boys. You looked very much the family pair—you and Dr Richard!'

'Only because we had domesticity thrust upon us,' said Kit, dropping a pile of folders and getting them all mixed up. 'Given a choice, I'd have much preferred to be less encumbered.'

'You mean, been alone with him?'

'I mean nothing of the sort.' Kit managed to laugh and bend down to her folders, hiding her give-away face. 'I saw the Libbots family there.' She changed the subject; she knew Megan was visiting Jill.

'Oh, yes, I saw them too, and Jill's thrilled to bits. They've got a house in Portsmouth, heard on Saturday that they can move in during the autumn. She never really liked that river bungalow, so I'm really pleased for her.'

'Yes,' Kit agreed, 'so am I. She'll be less lonely now.'

Megan helped her pick up her folders, and between them they sorted them out, just in time to see Richard's lean figure passing the outside window. 'Here he is; he's all yours!' Megan snapped her bag shut, and made for the door as Richard reached it, and, like the swinging Box and Cox, one went out while the other came in, with the briefest of greetings exchanged.

Richard's greeting of Kit was almost as brief, but she understood why this was. They had eight prospective mothers to see over the next two hours. She would be liaising with him in this: they would be working in partnership, working alongside one another. Professionalism would prevail at all times, and not once. . .not even once. . .would she dwell on personal longings. He would simply be the obstetrics GP and she the midwife-cum-nurse.

And, oh, boy, do we make a good team, she thought a little later on, when a diabetic who had been having hypoglycaemic attacks was shown in by one of the secretaries. Whilst Kit tested her specimen for sugar and albumen, Richard examined her, explaining that it would be best for her to go into hospital at thirty-two weeks, so that her diabetes could be stabilised prior to the birth of her child.

'Which will be by a Caesar at thirty-seven weeks. . . the midwife told me that!' Mrs Lane glared at Kit and Richard as though it were all their fault. 'Diabetes is more of a flaming nuisance than people realise!' was her parting shot before she joined her brow-mopping husband outside.

But the next patient—a girl with cardiac disease—was all smiles and optimism. 'Plenty of women with heart trouble have babies these days,' she informed Richard knowledgeably, as he listened to her chest.

'That's very true.' He was still listening, and wanted her to be quiet. Kit managed to silence her, by laying a finger over her lips. Folding his stethoscope, frowning a little, Richard enquired about breathlessness, examined her legs and ankles for swelling, read the report from the hospital cardiologist for the second time, and agreed with the patient when she told him that women with bad hearts had quick and easy labours.

'So there's always some compensation.' Her smile included Kit, who said she hoped she was managing to get in plenty of rest. 'Oh, I am,' she replied. 'And that's easier now, because we're living with my parents. We fell behind with our mortgage and our house was repossessed. Just now, though, I'm glad to be at home; it's lovely to be with Mum.' A beatific smile broadened her pale, puffy face. 'Everything that has happened so far seems to be meant.'

'Well, I just hope her husband thinks so,' Richard commented when she had gone. He drew in a deep breath and let it out, leaning back in his chair. 'How many more have we got, Kit?' He could see her back view through the curtains; she was changing the disposable sheet on the bed.

'Three.' She turned round, crumpling the used sheet into the bin. 'The multiple sclerosis who's in remission at present, Mrs Rolfe with persistent jaundice, and the middle-aged Mrs Dunn with a flare-up of her colitis.'

'I don't see their notes; they're not here.'

'Yes, they are.' Kit pointed them out, and in doing so noticed that Dinah James's papers were there. 'Mrs James isn't due this afternoon,' she said. 'She has no especial problems. . .has she?' she queried sharply, when she saw Richard's face.

'I got the notes out when they rang from the hospital. She's been admitted. I was going to tell you about it when we'd finished this afternoon. She's had a threatened miscarriage—fell in the High Street, was admitted by ambulance.'

'Haemorrhaging badly?' Kit's voice was low-pitched.

'I understand so, yes, but she's not having pains of the rhythmic type. She *may* not lose her child.'

'Is she dilated?'

'I'm told not.'

'How much blood has she lost?' Kit was rapping out questions, anxious for answers, although what she most wanted to do was rush off to the hospital to see Dinah for herself. She was one of *her* mothers, wasn't she. . .? She had managed her care up until now. . .and Dinah had been doing so well. 'Oh, stupid woman, why wasn't she more careful? Why couldn't she take proper care? I warned her about her attic stairs; now she has to fall in the street!' she burst out on a tide of anger, gnawing at her lip.

'I doubt if she did it on purpose——' Richard's bland voice steadied her '—and a large proportion of threatened miscarriages settle down with rest. But I don't have to tell *you* that, do I? Mrs James is in capable hands, so let's forget her for the moment and get the next patient in.'

In no way was this said dismissively, and the little

touch that alighted briefly on the back of Kit's hand made her realise that he sympathised with the way she was feeling, and that he minded about Dinah James, even though—being a man—he couldn't possibly understand how traumatic it was for a woman when something like this occurred. Now that was where a midwife had the edge on a male GP. I'll go and see Dinah as soon as I can, she thought, feeling slightly better, and even a little superior, as she called the next patient through.

She saw her next day during her lunch-break. Dinah was in Gynae Ward, which Kit was glad of, for to have been in Maternity wouldn't have been very kind. She had purple shadows under her eyes and no colour in her cheeks, but she was awake, having just had her lunch, when Kit appeared at her side. 'How are you feeling?' She pulled up a chair.

'Afraid to move in case something happens.' Dinah slewed her eyes to Kit; she was lying down, her spiky red hair draping the side of her cheek. 'They tell me the baby is unharmed, but do you think that's true? Perhaps they're just saying that. . .for the time being.'

'No, they never do that,' Kit told her without hesitation. 'I mean, what would be the point? They'd never lie about a thing like that. Women very often have threatened miscarriages, and, with proper rest and care, go through to their full term and have lovely babies.'

'I want mine. Now, isn't that odd? I mean, I didn't at first. It wasn't until this happened that I realised I'd been wanting him for weeks—ever since I stopped feeling so groggy, I suppose; perhaps even before that.'

'I've heard women say that before, Dinah.' Kit

smiled and was relieved to see Dinah grin, and go on to say,

'And there's another thing too, you know. I was terrified of hospitals. I didn't even want to go in one for just a matter of hours. Now, here I am, stuck here for maybe another week!'

'And you're not terrified?'

'Only about losing the kid. If everything's all right, if he stays put, I'll still have that domino thing. I don't want to alter that.' She was sleepy; she needed to rest. It was the ward's quiet time, anyway. Kit got up to go, 'Come again, won't you?' Dinah's eyes moved to hers again.

'Yes, of course I will.' Kit could see Sister, tall in the ward doorway. 'I'd better go before I'm thrown out, Dinah,' she smiled, and left the bed.

The following weekend was her long one off—all of Friday, Saturday and Sunday—so she saw Dinah on the Friday afternoon, and found her sitting up, doing some of her sewing. 'Now this looks more like it,' Kit said.

'I'm addicted to needle and thread!'

'So I see.'

'And I *am* all right, and so's the baby; isn't that marvellous? I'll be going home after the weekend.'

'Yes, Sister told me that, and it certainly is marvellous—couldn't be better, in fact.'

'Have a piece of Turkish delight,' Dinah said, passing Kit the box, and the two of them chatted till Dinah's husband, Bob, appeared at the start of visiting, carrying a sheaf of orange gladioli, and looking self-conscious, as he walked up the aisle of the long Nightingale Ward.

Soon after that Kit took her leave, and went down to see Josie, who was watching television in the day-room attached to the medical wards. She came out as soon as she saw Kit, and they went into her side-ward together. Josie looked fragile, but steady on her feet, and a little *distraite*, as though her thoughts were miles away, far removed from hospitals.

'I may be discharged on Wednesday,' she said, 'depending on the consultant. I shall know for certain on Monday, after he's done his round. I intend to go straight down to Eastbourne, you know, taking the boys. It'll only be days before they break up, so they won't be missing much school. You and your mother have been so good. . . I mean, having them like you did. We're both. . . I'm very grateful; they've been really happy with you.'

'They'll be happier with you; they're counting the days.' Kit was just about to ask if Mr Telford would be coming to Melbridge to fetch them all, when Richard came in, bent and kissed Josie, and said, 'No, Kit, please stay,' when she half rose, thinking that it might be tactful to leave.

'Without being rude to anyone,' Josie said, buffing her nails, 'I don't want any visitors tomorrow afternoon. I'm being taken down to the hairdressing salon on the second floor. I shall feel more human when my hair's clean—I can't stand it limp like this. So could you do something with the boys, Kit. . .? Explain to them how it is, and take them out, take their minds off it. . . You know what I mean?'

'Kit may have something else planned,' Richard said before Kit could speak.

'*Have* you?' Josie coloured a little.

'Well, as a matter of fact, the donkey sanctuary is having an open day tomorrow. It was evidently started in July 1970, which means it's twenty-one years old, and the Misses Cartwright are making a gala occasion of it. I thought I might take the boys there—they loved the donkeys on Saturday. There'll be rides at special prices, which will all help with the funds.'

'Or we could take them to the zoo—the boys, not the donkeys!' Richard was looking at Kit.

'To Regent's Park?' She couldn't keep the astonishment out of her voice.

'Yes, why not?' Richard's brows rose, while a smile broadened his face. 'I'm not on call tomorrow, so there'd be no need to rush.'

'The twins have been to the zoo,' remarked Josie. 'Paul took them last year. Still, they can't have seen it all, can they? And, as there's all this talk of closing it down, maybe they should go again while they've got the chance.' She was gabbling, Kit noticed, and pleating the sash on her dressing-gown. Why did she feel so much discomfiture when mentioning Paul? It was unlike her to be so unworldly. Richard knew about Paul, knew she'd been married to him, that he had access to his sons. Still, Josie had been very ill, hadn't she, and this might have made her extra-sensitive about everything.

'The zoo sounds a good idea to me.' Kit tried the effect of a smile, tried to break through the embarrassment that hung about the prim little room. 'I've not been for about ten years, and that was with a school party.'

'Oh, yes, I remember, and I didn't go,' Josie reminisced. 'I was laid up with flu; it was mid-March and cold as charity.'

It wasn't as cold as charity next day, but neither was it too hot. It was exactly right for walking great distances from elephants to giraffes, from nocturnal rodents to seals and walruses, and into the reptile house, where the weather didn't matter, anyway, and where the chief attraction for Daniel and Harry was a log-like crocodile lying halfway out of his pool.

'If he could burst through the glass, would he eat us all up?' Daniel asked, amusing the semi-circle of people standing just behind.

'He might eat our lunch, but not us,' Kit said, feeling Harry press close to her side.

'But he can't get out, can he, Kit?' he enquired anxiously.

'Not a chance, Harry.' Richard bent to him. 'I think his main diet is fishes. You remember that little rhyme in *Alice* about the lazy crocodile?

How cheerfully he seems to grin
How neatly spreads his claws,
And welcomes little fishes in
With gently smiling jaws.

'Yes, and he *is* smiling, isn't he? I can see his teeth.' Partly reassured, but not entirely happy, Harry asked to see the bears. 'The white ones on the rocks that sometimes look dirty.'

'I want to see the lions; the lions are best!' Daniel, who was over-excited, started to lead the way out.

'We'll see the polar bears *and* the lions,' said Richard, 'but not until we've had lunch.'

'I second that.' Kit smiled at him, grateful for the respite. She was beginning to flag and becoming oppressed by the aquatic semi-darkness of the reptile house and the sight of so many horny amphibians.

The light and fresh air outside was welcome, so was

the much-trodden patch of unoccupied grass on which they sat and spread out the picnic feast. Mrs Greenham had packed a variety of sandwiches, cheese and biscuits, sausage rolls, strawberry shortcake, big juicy peaches, and bananas for the boys. Richard fetched drinks from a stall—Coke for the twins, and surprisingly good coffee in paper cups for himself and Kit. It was a good picnic, a splendid picnic, every morsel and crumb tasting ambrosial eaten there in the heart of London, under a midsummer English sky, the air full of jungle sounds.

'Your mother is nothing less than a marvel.' Kneeling on the grass, closing the empty picnic basket, Richard looked over at Kit. He thought she had never looked more enticing, in her yellow printed dress. She was sitting bolt upright, clasping her knees, her golden bell of hair moving forwards when she dipped her head, sifting on her neck as she watched the twins scampering off to a distant litter-bin.

He moved closer to her, and she felt his gaze; they were close enough to kiss. She knew that if she turned to him that was what would happen. It wouldn't happen unless she moved; if she kept quite still like this, staring ahead, watching the twins, nothing would happen. The twins had found something on the pavement—perhaps a beetle or a ladybird. They were squatting down, completely absorbed. 'Something has captured their interest, and that's for sure,' she said.

'I know the feeling.' His voice had a throb; it awakened one in her. Almost without volition she turned and parted her lips for his kiss. When it came, when they joined, when their breath intermingled, when she felt the shift of his palm over her breasts, she thought she would die of the sharply honed, exquisite pleasure that was thrusting her to the skies.

But she was still on earth when the kiss ended. The sun was still shining, and the twins were still pavement-engrossed; everything was the same. 'We're forgetting our charges, aren't we?' Richard drew her to her feet, holding her hands, looking down at her, his face darkly flushed.

'Someone could have kidnapped them!' Kit sounded as breathless as he.

'I don't thing we've been away long enough for that!' A smile tugged at his mouth, and together they went over to where Daniel and Harry were crouched.

'We've got a furry caterpillar,' Daniel said excitedly. 'It keeps looping itself up. Look, Kit, it's a caterpillar; we learned about them at school.'

'It keeps looping itself up,' Harry affirmed.

'Yes, I can see that it does. Now you can do the same.' Richard's voice was firm. 'Loop yourselves up, and put the poor thing back in the grass, or someone will squash it flat.'

They did as he said without argument; they could recognise authority when they heard it. Kit felt quite sorry for them. After all, it was *their* outing, and Richard had sounded so stern. 'Let's make the afternoon a really good one for them,' she said, looking up at him.

He took her point at once. 'We will,' he promised. 'I've absolutely no right to take my frustrations out on them. We'll make it an afternoon-plus.'

He was as good as his word. For the next two hours the twins had the time of their lives. They were lifted, in turn, up on his shoulders to see the polar bears. The crowd was dense, for the bears were popular, especially as there was a baby one, which drew oohs and aahs from the crowd. The lions weren't so willing to be seen; only one showed herself.

In the end it was the monkeys who interested the boys the most. They spent nearly an hour watching their antics, and being deafened by their yammering cries. They saw the hippos and the rhinos, and fed the elephants. They went into the parrot house and were deafened again, and they saw an eagle, and finally the humming-birds. Harry was enchanted with the latter. 'Is it them singing?' he asked.

'No, it's the rapid movement of their wings that makes the humming noise.' Watching Richard as he bent to the child, Kit fancied he looked more relaxed. He had mentioned 'frustrations'. Well, she had them too, which was precisely why being together with Josie ill in hospital was highly dangerous.

Tea was drunk, ice-cream was consumed, and then it was time to go. Richard was all for getting a taxi back to Waterloo. They had had one this morning, but this time the twins clamoured to go on the Tube. Seeing Richard's hesitation, Daniel seized the advantage. '*Daddy* took us back by Tube, when we came here last year.'

'Emotional blackmail, no less!' Richard said to Kit, as, with a twin firmly anchored to each of them, they began the longish walk to the Underground station. 'I just hope you're not as footsore as I am, Kit.'

'Oh, I expect we'll both live!' She was wearing flatties, and just as well, she thought.

'Are you off duty tomorrow too?'

'Yes.'

'So am I.'

It was bat-and-ball conversation like this, interrupted by questions from the tireless twins, that got them to the Underground station and down into its stirring, stale-smelling depths. Their train should, via a series of stops, have gone straight through to Waterloo, but, for some reason, when it reached Oxford Circus everyone was told to get out. '*All* change. . .*All* change!' a railway official intoned, walking the length of the platform to make sure that he was obeyed.

So once more Kit and Richard and the two little boys found themselves part of a densely packed crowd, while the now empty train trickled its way out of the station into the tunnel beyond. Bodies pressed against bodies, and the pressure increased as more people surged in from street level. 'Stick as close as you can!' Richard, who was carrying the children's coats and the picnic basket, tried his best to help Kit. She was holding the children against her front, an arm over each of their shoulders; their backs were towards her, their feet trampling hers. It was less than comfortable. People were grumbling, and a baby who sounded new-born was yelling its head off close behind her ear.

'Why doesn't another train come?' Harry asked, just as a distant vibrating rumble signalled the approach of one.

'It's coming now.'

And come it did, rollicking out of the tunnel, pouring alongside the platform—a blur of windows and faces—till it stopped, and they saw it was packed to the doors. 'Good heavens, we'll never get on it!' Richard said, as the doors drew apart. 'We'll stay where we are. . .right where we are! We can't sardine in there!'

Kit agreed with him, for of course they couldn't, not with the children in tow; but a great many people went for it, and the thrust from behind was hard to withstand, even with Richard acting as a bulwark for her and the twins. And for a time the train just stood there, doing nothing, its doors open wide. Richard and 'family' were at the edge of the platform, so could see all the people inside. 'It'll pull out in a minute; there'll soon be another,' Kit heard him say. . .at the same time as the doors started closing. . .at the same time as Daniel tore out of her grasp with a shout of, 'Daddy' and was through and on to the train in the split-second before the doors shut and it moved off with a jolt.

'Danny, no. . . Danny. . .*Danny*!' Kit heard herself screaming out to the packed carriages that were passing them, aware that Richard was banging on the sides of the train to try to get someone inside to pull the communication cord or perhaps alert the guard. But they didn't, or couldn't; it was to no avail. The train rocketed on and he had to stand back until the end of it flicked by like the snap of a blind, and into the tunnel, leaving Kit and him staring at one another in frozen horror. What on earth were they going to do?

Harry started to cry, and Kit bent to him, just as a draught of warm air and a distant murmur heralded the arrival of yet another train. The sound galvanised Richard into action. 'We'll get on this, get out at the first stop, in the hope that he'll be there. . .hope that he'll have the sense to get out and wait for us.' His words were a shout as the train roared in, and the crowd started pushing again.

'It'll be Piccadilly, and I'm sure he won't. . .' Kit had no time to finish, for they were moving forward on to the train, she clutching Harry, Richard trying to save them both from being knocked to the floor.

They hung on to a strap in the train and once more she tried to protest. 'Danny won't think to get out of the train. . .he won't know what to do! When he finds out it wasn't his father, and of course it couldn't have been, he'll be terrified. He won't know what to do. . . he's only a little boy!'

'It may have been his father, in which case he'll be safe. Brett'll have the sense to get out and wait for us to appear. He'll wait with Daniel,' Richard emphasised, but his face was tense and Kit could see the glisten of sweat on his upper lip.

'Paul Brett is abroad. He's in France, Richard—that's what I'm trying to tell you! Danny must have seen someone like him—a black-bearded man—but it wasn't Paul. . .*couldn't* have been Paul! Did you see Daddy on that other train?' she asked a tearful Harry, knowing that she was verging on panic, and trying to bank it down.

'Daddy's in France.' Harry echoed her words, rubbing his face in her skirt.

They were approaching Piccadilly; white-tiled walls and black cables slid past. Richard sagged at the knees, trying to see out of the nearest window. His next words amazed Kit, but gave her a chink of hope. 'He could be in London; he was due here in June or July,' he said, watching the doors drawing apart, putting an arm about Kit and Harry, and getting them safely out.

'Are you sure?'

'Yes.'

They couldn't talk much for once again they found

themselves in a forest of people, even more dense than before. 'Which way?' Kit gasped.

'We'll stand where we are till the crowd thins a bit.' Richard stooped and picked Harry up, handing Kit the coats and basket. She took them, feeling sick, and, in spite of the heat, cold to her very bones.

'If we don't find him?' She plucked at his sleeve.

'We'll get the police on to it,' he said, stiff-faced, 'but I still think we're going to find him here.'

She wondered if he was as confident as he sounded, or if his optimism was assumed for Harry's benefit, even, perhaps, for hers. He must have known she was blaming herself for not having grasped Daniel more tightly. The child had taken her by surprise, but that was no excuse. It was her fault. She went even more cold, as though she were turning to ice.

It was impossible to see in front of them; too many people hemmed them in. Where was Daniel. . .where was he? She wanted to shout his name. Wherever he was he'd be frightened; he wouldn't know what to do. And the thought of his terror was awful—he was only a little boy.

'Force a way through; push through!' Richard shouted above her head. 'That way, towards the "WAY OUT" sign. My guess is—' The rest of his sentence was drowned by the clatter of the train pulling out, but the crowd had thinned—at least for the moment—and Kit could see her feet. Richard set Harry down, and, holding his hands, they walked in a line towards the exit sign.

He wouldn't be there. Kit was sure of that; she was without a shred of hope. It was unlike Richard to act on a hunch; they ought to be ringing the police. She was so sure they were on a wild-goose chase, and that Daniel was miles away, that when she saw him—saw a little boy in butcher-blue shorts, standing by the exit archway, holding the hand of a tall, dark-bearded man—she thought it was a mirage. It wasn't until Richard and Harry shouted in chorus, 'There he is!' that the mirage became reality, and she burst into tears as she stood.

It was through tears that she saw Harry run to his father, saw him lift him up in his arms, saw Daniel running towards her and Richard, heard Richard say, 'Kit, it's all right,' heard Daniel saying, 'Daddy thought you'd come and find me here!'

By then they had all converged, and Paul Brett was greeting Kit. 'You haven't changed; I'd have known you anywhere.' He bent and kissed her cheek.

'I'd have known you too,' Kit said with truth, for he hadn't changed very much. He was still a handsome pirate with his neat black beard, teeth very white, brows formidable, meeting over his nose.

She introduced him to Richard, wondering how they would feel, meeting at last. Richard had always been curious about Paul, which was natural enough, while Paul, in his turn, must surely have wondered what his successor was like.

Neither of them said very much, at least not at first. They were looking at the twins, who were grinning at one another in a sheepish kind of way. Harry's love for his brother was touchingly apparent as he told him solemnly, 'We thought you'd been taken away by a bad man, and that we'd never see you again.'

Paul Brett shifted his gaze to Richard. Both men were the same height, and their eyes were dead level as he said, 'You evidently guessed I'd get out here and wait for you at the exit.'

'It's what I would have done had the position been reversed.' Richard sounded a little clipped.

'A case, I think, of two great minds thinking alike.'

Richard nodded. 'I expect you saw us on the platform at Oxford Circus.'

'I saw the whole performance.' They kept on talking, but Kit couldn't hear any more. Another train had arrived, and more passengers were cutting a swath between them and her. She moved back against the wall, holding tightly to the twins, trying to keep the men in view. They'd be talking about Josie. Daniel would have been bound to have told Paul about her illness. . .about her being in hospital, and all the rest.

When he said goodbye to them a few minutes later, he told the twins he would see them soon. 'Yes, *very* soon, I promise.' He kissed Kit as well, muttered something about an appointment in Regent Street, nodded at Richard, quite affably but without shaking hands, and then was off, turning the corner, and disappearing from view.

'He could have come home with us,' Daniel remarked to no one in particular.

'No, he couldn't; he's busy,' Harry pointed out.

'Still, we saw him, didn't we?'

'Yes, we saw him.' They chattered like monkeys on the tube to Waterloo, but it wasn't until they were on the train for Melbridge that Richard said much to Kit.

CHAPTER NINE

IT WAS the five o'clock train, so fairly full, but even so they managed to find a clutch of four seats—Richard and Kit sitting side by side, the twins opposite.

'Our outing didn't lack drama, did it?' Richard remarked, giving Kit the chance to ask how he'd known Paul Brett was in London. 'Josie told me around Easter-time that he was due again in July.' He got up to open the window a crack. It was very hot in the train.

'And I suppose,' Kit prompted, 'Daniel told him about her being ill.'

'He knew about Jo's illness right from the first; the Telfords let him know, so he's just told me. I didn't know before. I expect they thought he ought to be told in case she didn't pull through. He would have wanted some say about the boys then. I expect that was in their minds.'

'Thank goodness things didn't come to that!' Kit stared over at the boys.

'As you say, thank goodness.' There was silence, then Richard said, 'He saw her in hospital twice, apparently, once when she was in ICU, once when she was out.'

'Did he?' Kit sounded incredulous.

'That's what he said.'

'I find that difficult to believe.'

'I wonder why?' Richard's mouth was tight.

'Well, because Josie would have told me. I know she would, even if she'd kept it from you. What I mean is,' she corrected quickly, seeing his brows go up, 'she might have felt awkward about telling you, but she would have mentioned it to me.'

'You think so?'

'I do.' But, even as she said this, she began to have creeping doubts. Josie might not have confided in her; she could be secretive at times. . . As I can, when it suits me, she thought with a pang of guilt. They were beyond the schoolgirl stage when they told one another all. 'Well, if he did visit her,' she went on carefully, 'I can understand why, I think. They were husband and wife at one time; there must be *some* feeling left. He probably saw her right at the start of her illness when she didn't know anyone, so she might not know he's been at all, which is why it never came up.'

'What a loyal friend!' He turned his head, which brought their faces close. Was he being sarcastic. . .*was* he? She could read nothing in his eyes—slate-grey eyes, deepening to black. 'That's the last thing I am,' she said thickly, turning her head away.

They were drawing into Richmond, slowing and stopping; more passengers were getting on. The twins had to give up their seats and sit between Richard and Kit, which in no way pleased them; they were restless and over-tired.

'Can we play I Spy?' Daniel asked. 'Just Harry and me.' Richard said they could, if they were quiet about it and didn't make rude and personal remarks about people sitting near.

The game got going and flourished all the way to Feltham and beyond, causing amusement to the

American couple sitting opposite, especially when Harry, looking mysterious, spied with his little eye something beginning with S, which turned out to be 'snore', coming from an elderly man just across the aisle.

'You're a lovely family.' The American woman leaned forward and tapped Kit's knee. 'So *English*, so British! It's great to see it, you know.'

Neither Kit nor Richard denied the relationship. Why bother to explain to perfect strangers whom they could never see again?

The train was approaching Melbridge Station, and Richard was reaching for the coats. Kit was suddenly aware of her own weariness, even more so of Richard's mood. The fright of temporarily losing Daniel had run them both ragged, of course, and then there had been all that business with Paul. What *exactly* had he said to Richard to make him so withdrawn?

'We evidently looked the picture of domestic bliss back there in the train,' he said a few minutes later as they walked over the iron bridge.

'Appearances can be deceptive!' She was rattled by his tone.

'You could have set Mrs Texas right.'

'So could you!' Were they bickering?

'I couldn't be bothered.'

'Neither could I.'

Yes, they *were* bickering, and how horrible it was, how hateful! Angry tears stung Kit's eyes, which was why she didn't see Andrew Gordon standing by his car, scanning the passengers on the bridge, till she heard Richard say, 'I spy with my little eye someone beginning with A.'

'Why, it's Andrew!' She waved; so did the twins.

'He's come to give you a lift.'

'Couldn't be better!' They were going down the steps, and Andrew was coming to meet them, his fawn hair and light suit looking yellow in the sun. He also looked pleased with himself, smiling straight at Kit.

'I thought I'd come and meet you, as you hadn't got your car. There's a queue for taxis, so you'd have had to wait.' He nodded over the road. 'And that includes you too, of course, Richard. I can drop you off *en route*.'

'Thank you, that's helpful; we're all pretty tired,' Richard said pleasantly. So into the Citroën they all climbed—Kit in the back with a twin on either side of her, Richard in the front.

'How did you know which train we'd be on?' Kit caught hold of Harry, who rolled, giggling, over her lap, as they turned down into the town.

'I didn't, but you said about half-five.' Andrew braked at the lights. 'And as I was here in Melbridge anyway, choosing wallpaper for the house, I thought it would be worthwhile meeting a couple of trains. Actually, I hadn't long arrived when I saw you on the bridge.'

'Good timing!'

'Brilliant!' Richard intoned from the front.

'How was the zoo?' Andrew's eyes met Kit's in the driving-mirror.

'Crowded.'

'Being Saturday, it would be. Oh, by the way, Kit——' he slackened speed to crawl behind a bus '—see what you think about the wallpaper; it's down there by your feet.'

Kit knew it was; she'd been trying to stop Daniel kicking it. She lifted up a roll and inspected it through the Cellophane wrapping. 'Looks very good; it'll be right for the hall, make it seem much lighter.'

'Yes, that's what I thought, and with white paint. . .' They had got rid of the bus, and Andrew was asking Richard where he wanted to be dropped. 'I expect you're going home now, aren't you?'

'No, to the hospital, thanks, but if you put me down in the High Street it's no distance from there.'

Kit saw Richard's arm move to unsnib his belt, then stop as Andrew said, 'I'll take you to the hospital; it's no bother.' Round the corner they went and up the hill, the twins wanting to know if they could see their mother.

'Not tonight, boys, no,' Richard said firmly, but kindly enough. He threw a quick glance over his shoulder at Kit. 'You'll be able to see her tomorrow.'

'Of course—tomorrow afternoon, immediately after lunch,' she promised, then fell to wondering what Richard was going to say to Josie now. . .tonight. . . when he went up to her room. He would tell her all about Daniel's escapade, and meeting Paul in the Underground. He would ask her about his visiting her, and why she'd not mentioned it. He wouldn't upset her, for that wasn't his style, and she was still an invalid, but he would want to know why she had held out on him, and this Kit could understand. Why, even *she* felt faintly miffed that Josie hadn't told her.

At Andrew's suggestion, when they got to the hospital, she moved into the front seat, leaving the twins, now half asleep, lolling together in the back. 'They look like a pair of book-ends,' Richard said, his expression unreadable, his movements jerky as he straightened up at the kerb.

Richard's step, Kit thought, as he crossed the yard, had a lagging quality. He didn't want to be at odds with Josie, perhaps uncover hurtful truths. Not that he had anything to worry about, for Josie would explain, and it would all be nothing, or nothing much, and they'd have a good laugh together. It was necessary to have it out, but it would come right in the end.

And, because Kit truly believed this, she was very taken aback when she took the twins in to see Josie next day and found not Richard but Paul Brett sitting in her room. Josie turned a smiling face in her direction, while the boys rushed at their father. 'We didn't know you'd be *here*, Daddy! You didn't tell us, Kit!'

'Kit didn't know,' Paul told them, watching Josie scoop Daniel up.

'You must never run off like that again, Danny; it was frightening for everyone.' Josie was sitting out of bed in her blue velvet robe, her newly washed hair cut to shoulder-length, falling in shallow waves. There were other changes too, and Kit marvelled at them. Her skin had a glow, her eyes were shining, and her mouth smiling; gone was her invalid look. What was going on? What was happening? Kit looked from her to Paul, saw them exchange glances, saw a signal of some kind pass.

'I'll take the boys out for half an hour, leave you two to talk.' Paul shooed them into the corridor, cautioning them to be quiet. 'This is a hospital, not a playground. Once you get outside and into the park you can make all the hullabaloo you like.'

Kit couldn't wait for them to be gone, couldn't wait

for the door to be closed. 'Whatever is going *on*, Jo?' The question burst out of her.

'I'm going back to Paul,' Josie said simply, watching her friend's face. 'We're going to get married all over again; we still love one another.'

'Good *lord*!' Kit gaped.

'There's no need to look so shocked!'

'But what about. . .?' She was struggling to speak.

'I told Richard last night.' Josie's smile slipped a little. 'I didn't enjoy it much. Paul and I were going to tell him together, here, this afternoon, but that business on the Underground brought Richard in here last night. You see, Mum and Dad sent for Paul when I was dangerously ill. He came, but had to return to France almost immediately, but he came again when I was *compos mentis*, and asked me to marry him. I accepted straight away; there was no doubt in my mind.'

'You were. . .engaged. . .to Richard!' Could this be true? Was she hearing right?

'I know that,' Josie said quietly, 'and I thought it would work out. We weren't madly in love, but we both wanted marriage, and we got along just fine. Well, when I say that, we had our ups and downs, but then most couples have those. Richard was always lovely to me, and terrific with the boys. The thing was, when we got engaged, when Paul got to hear about it, he was angry, really furious. He was jealous, of course.'

'You were divorced; it was nothing to do with him!'

'People can't help how they feel. Anyway, he wanted to keep seeing me, apart from the access thing with the boys.'

'And you *agreed*?' Kit's voice rose up.

'Yes, I couldn't help myself. Ever since Easter,

whenever he was in England I went to London to see him.'

'I see.' Kit's mind tracked backwards, remembering occasions when Josie's trips to town had been frequent, but had been explained away as shopping expeditions, or meeting up with her parents. 'So you were going up to town when the boys were at school, seeing Paul on the quiet?' She heard the blame in her voice; she felt angry for Richard. . .for Richard. . .for Richard, who would now be free, wouldn't he. . .*who was no longer engaged*!

'If you like to put it that way, yes.' Josie sounded unabashed.

'You seem to have forgotten that Paul walked out on you four years ago.' Kit said the words, while the thought kept persisting. . . Richard was free.

'I don't blame him for that. I was hell to live with, and he didn't abandon us. He was generous where money was concerned, and he *gave* me the house. He thought the world of the twins and he hated only seeing them in spurts. Most of the break-up was my fault; I always knew it was.' Josie was bent on whitewashing Paul. 'This time it'll work,' she said.

'I hope so.' Oh, Richard, my love, what are you feeling now?

'Surely you can wish us happiness?' Josie shook back her hair. 'Mum and Dad are over the moon; they think it's the right thing. Surely you can try to be. . .enthusiastic. You're supposed to be my friend.'

'Oh, Jo.' Kit responded to that at once. 'Oh, Jo, of course I'm glad, of course I wish you happiness, and you *know* that we're friends!' It was an emotional moment, and even Richard slipped out of Kit's mind—

at least for a second or two—as she hugged and kissed her friend. 'I just hope,' she cautioned, 'that you're still going to Eastbourne to convalesce, for you're not up to full strength yet, not by a very long chalk.'

'Oh, I am. I mean, I'll be going to Eastbourne. Paul will be taking me, as soon as I get out of here, as soon as I get my discharge. He's taking the whole of his annual leave; we're getting married down there. Afterwards we'll be living in London till the beginning of September, and then, Kit—wait for it; wait until you hear this—we're going to live in America, in New York, for two or three years! The boys will go to day-school there. Now what do you think about that?'

'I'm winded; I'm speechless!'

'Exciting, isn't it?'

'Oh, Jo, you *will* take care?'

'Paul will do that; he'll take care of all of us.' Josie's eyes were soft.

'How will the boys take it, I wonder?'

'Oh, like me, of course. They'll be ecstatic, thrilled to bits, especially as we'll be going to America on the QE2. Paul insisted on that; he says he's not risking me on a plane just yet. He'll be telling the twins all this now, explaining everything to them. It's going to be all right, Kit; I feel it deep down. Paul was the first and only man I've ever truly loved.'

Paul Brett came back with his sons, and it was as Josie had said. They were ecstatic, literally jigging up and down. 'We're going to Nanna's first, and then to London, and then to *America*! Perhaps we'll go to Disneyland, and see the real Mickey Mouse!' They stood in front of Kit, shoulder to shoulder, two little look-alike boys, and she felt a shaft of what could have been sadness, for how quick they were to adapt. How easily they could throw off the old, and go forward to the new, providing—she watched them go over to Josie—their mother wasn't far away.

Soon after that she took them off, back to Ford House. They made no protest, for they were all agog to tell Aunt Green their news. They were also anxious not to miss out on the special Sunday tea that she always prepared for them. 'Daddy's bought Mummy a new ring; he showed it to us in its little box,' Harry told Kit, hanging on to the back of her seat in the car, and blowing down her neck. 'I expect he's giving it to her now.'

'Yes, perhaps he is,' Kit said, thinking of Richard, for what must he be feeling?

Mrs Greenham's comment was that it was all for the best—Josie was doing the right thing for herself and the children too. 'Not that I agree with the way she's gone about it, deceiving Richard like that, but then she's never been open and above-board—that's not her way. As for Richard, fond though he is of the children, they'll be better with their own father, especially as he's a loving father; there's nothing much wrong with Paul Brett. The pity of it is that he and Josie didn't try a little harder to make things work out in the first place, then there wouldn't have been all that. . .hiatus, which upset everyone.'

'Friendship is the only thing that matters in marriage,' Andrew said when he heard. 'This "in love" romantic business simply doesn't last.'

Kit didn't agree—at least not entirely—but she didn't say so, for, remembering Andrew's broken romance, she felt he was bound to be disenchanted where sexual love was concerned.

Next morning all she could think of when she called at the health centre was how Richard might be feeling, and whether she would run into him. She saw him, but in the distance only, talking to Dr Foxley. She hoped he might look up and see her sifting through her tray, but one of the social workers joined him and they went into the consulting room.

She did three postnatal visits before lunch, then stopped to buy sandwiches before going to the health centre office to eat them there. Again, she hoped to see Richard, or hear something about him, but no one mentioned him and she could only suppose that as Josie hadn't worked there since Christmas interest in the two of them might have waned. It was even possible she supposed, that the news hadn't filtered through, for Richard would hardly make an announcement of it. . . there was no reason why he should.

She saw him when she was leaving and preparing to get back into her car. He came across to her, walking swiftly in the fine mizzle of rain that had been falling in fits and starts ever since breakfast-time. 'Josie will have told you of our break-up, I'm sure?' He lost no time in coming straight to the point, which was always his way.

'She told me yesterday.' Kit, too, was direct. 'I was very surprised.' She tried to say the conventional 'Sorry', but couldn't get her tongue round the word, or wouldn't, or didn't want to, for sorry was the last thing she was.

'Surprised, were you?' His gaze deepened, and she thought she saw doubt in his eyes, and reacted against it in stark dismay.

'You can't possibly think that I knew what was going on! I didn't; I had no idea!' She made herself very plain.

'Sorry, I shouldn't have said that, should I?' She felt his hand on her shoulder. She was wearing her cape, which was heat-making, but had the merit of keeping her dry.

'No, I don't think you should.' She smiled as she said this, taking the sting from her words. He smiled back and in a flash they were close, communicating wordlessly, standing there in the puddly tarmac yard.

'Better hop in; you're getting wet.' He opened the car door.

'Did you want me for anything else?' she asked, certain that he did, for he wasn't moving off in his usual rapid way.

'Oh, yes, to ask if I can come over to Ford House tomorrow evening. I'd like to say goodbye to the twins. Josie's discharge has been confirmed for Wednesday, so that will be departure date for the Brett family. I've already said goodbye to Jo.' He looked, Kit thought, more embarrassed than upset. All this couldn't be easy for him.

'Of course you can come; the boys will expect it. Come any time you like; we'll all be pleased to see you,' she ended in a rush. His embarrassment had conveyed itself to her, making them both avoid eye contact and feel uncomfortable before she quickly drove off.

Her first antenatal call that afternoon was out at Crayton, and as she drove there in the now pouring rain she wondered how Richard *really* felt about his break-up with Josie and the boys. Josie had stressed that they'd never been madly in love. She had also implied that Richard had been wriggling on the hook for some time. But was this really the case, Kit wondered, or had Josie said it, or implied it, to excuse her deception with Paul? He had kissed her on Saturday with passion and fervour; he had wanted her ardently then. . .as she had him. She shivered, recalling the way her body had sung, the way her senses had sharpened and leapt to match his own. Did he. . .would he ever love her? She didn't want an affair; she wanted him for keeps, for ever and a day. She wanted to marry him.

There were workmen repairing the old farmhouse up on Coombe Rise. Kit had to slow down behind their vans, which turned up a mud-churned lane opposite her patient's house. What a day to work outside, especially on a roof!

'It's being got ready for holiday lets,' Kathleen Revett told her. 'Hardly anyone's trying to sell houses these days; it takes too long.'

'I suppose so.' Kit wasn't all that interested; she was checking Kathleen's pulse. Next she examined her abdomen and listened to the foetal heart. 'Couldn't be better; you've got a strong baby in there.' She smiled and straightened up. Kathleen, in her third trimester, was booked for a domino delivery. She was one of Richard's patients and knew Dinah James from the clinic. She asked Kit how she was.

'I heard about her fall, and that she was in hospital. Is she going to be all right?'

'Thankfully, yes.' Kit folded her stethoscope. 'Both she and the baby. Any day now I'm expecting to hear that she's been discharged home.'

'I'm glad.' Kathleen looked down at herself, and put

a hand on her bulge. 'I'm getting awfully twitchy, you know, even with nine weeks to go. Ian doesn't help by watching me about and asking if I'm all right.'

'Oh, dear, that's men for you, but you're fine,' Kit laughed. 'In a little over two months your daughter will be here, and then we'll all celebrate.' Kathleen was one of the mothers-to-be who had wanted to know the sex of her child from the ultrasound scan. When she was told she was carrying a daughter, she couldn't have been more pleased.

When Kit went in to see Josie that evening she found her sitting by her bed, busily making lists of all the things she had to do. 'There's so *much* to arrange, Kit,' she said, pushing back her hair. 'Of course Paul is doing most of it; he's brilliant at organising.'

'What's been organised so far?' Kit asked, sitting down on the bed.

'Masses,' Josie giggled, then went on to say, 'We're getting married three weeks on Thursday at the Eastbourne register office. We're not inviting anyone at all, except Mum and Dad and the twins. I'm telling you this so that you won't feel hurt when you don't get an invite. Paul's parents were invited, but they can't come because they'll be on holiday then. Paul is staying with them at the moment, you know, and commuting up to town. They're very pleased about everything and have written to tell me so. I'm so happy, Kit, I could burst with it! I feel things have come right at last.'

Her happiness was infectious, and the two girls gripped hands and laughed. 'Richard came in to say goodbye,' Josie went on to say, the faintest of pink tingeing her cheeks as her eyes slid away from Kit's. 'He wished us luck as well,' she averred, then quickly changed tack and asked when Andrew was moving into his house.

'He thinks in roughly three weeks' time, perhaps on your wedding-day.' Kit was thinking about Richard again. How did he *really* feel about all these rapid arrangements in which he had no part? With an effort she brought her attention back to Josie's question about Andrew. 'Before you ask, Jo, I'm not moving in with him,' she said.

'Not even on a hands-off basis?'

'On no basis at all.'

'Don't you want to move back to Melbridge? I mean, you must be sick of motoring in from Grantford each day, and it'll be worse when the winter comes.'

'I'd like to be nearer my base, yes,' Kit admitted. 'Mother knows I'm on the look-out for something, but so far I've had no luck.'

'You could rent my house,' Josie said, so smartly that Kit stared at her open-mouthed.

'Good heavens, Josie!'

'You can if you like. You see, I'm not going to sell. Paul thinks it's the wrong time. He's advised me to rent it out—let it on a monthly basis, for perhaps the next two years. We shall be taking some of the furniture, but there'll still be enough left to call it a furnished tenancy. We thought it fair to ask. . .' She quoted a rent which wasn't unreasonable. 'So what do you say?' She finished a trifle anxiously, looking over at her friend.

'Oh, Jo, I don't know. . . I'm not sure.' Kit was too surprised to decide.

'Well, think about it until tomorrow, and then let me know. If you don't want the whole house, you could let part of it off. I wouldn't mind that, not in the least, because I know you'd look after it.'

Paul Brett arrived then, and Kit left soon after, but long before she reached home she knew she was going to accept Josie's offer; it was too good to refuse. Russell Road was near to the health centre *and* the hospital base, which gave it the edge on Ford House and Grantford any day of the week. After all, it wouldn't always be summer, and on dark winter evenings, after a long and tiring day, she wouldn't exactly relish an extra two-mile drive on roads that might be covered in ice.

Mrs Greenham was quick to see this, and agreed it made sense to accept. 'Go for it, Kit, but only if it's what *you* want,' she stressed. 'Don't do it to oblige Josie; you've done that often enough.'

She would be nearer Richard—that fact hadn't escaped Kit, of course. His house wasn't near Russell Road, but they would be in the same town, using the same shops and amenities. They would be almost bound to bump into one another from time to time, quite aside from their work. All manner of delicious possibilities showered Kit like rain. In no way, no way now was she going to change her job. She didn't have to, did she? There was no reason why she should. There was every reason for her to stay exactly where she was. I love you, Richard. . . I love you, I love you. . .and perhaps, in time, you'll love me.

In the face of all this anticipation Mrs Greenham's next comment was anticlimactic. 'You'll be near Andrew,' she remarked comfortably. 'That will be nice for both of you; you can help each other out.'

It was just on eight-thirty when Richard arrived at

Ford House next evening. He was all apologies. 'I was called out to an RTA,' he explained. 'I'd have rung if I could.' He was speaking to Kit, who had been on the listen for his car since the end of surgery time.

'GPs' and policemen's jobs excuse them anything,' she said. 'I had to get the boys to bed, as they've a long drive tomorrow, but they're awake and waiting to see you.'

'They know I bear gifts,' he smiled. Kit could see the gifts, which were probably books, lodged against his chest, while his other hand still grasped his bag. She gently relieved him of this, their fingers touching as the small exchange was made. Each looked at the other across the small distance no thicker than a hand—a distance that was nothing to two people who wanted to kiss and hold. She couldn't be feeling all this on her own; it just wasn't possible. He *does* like me; he feels *something* for me; he'll turn to me in the end. These were her thoughts as she stood in the hall and watched him mount the stairs. It was best, she felt, to let him see the twins alone, for he'd have things to say to them, special things; he might even tell them a story for the last time. Being Richard, he would keep his goodbyes as casual and as devoid of drama as possible. He loved the boys and he would never upset them, not in a million years.

He was up there for about half an hour, during which time Kit and her mother got a cold meal ready for him on a tray, but he was no sooner coming down the stairs than Harry called Kit up to them. 'He wants to know if you've packed his dinosaur stickers,' Richard told her as they passed.

She had, but neither child was ready for sleep. Their

new books—the ones Richard had brought them—had to be packed straight away. A dozen questions had to be answered, and it was a good ten minutes later before Kit could extricate herself and get back downstairs. She was surprised to see her mother and Richard still talking in the hall. 'We've got some supper for you, Richard; you're supposed to be eating it.' She looked from him to her mother, then back again at him, as she saw him shake his head.

'As I've just explained to your mother,' he said, 'I really can't stop. I'm anxious about the accident victim. I want to call in at the accident unit and see how he is.' He stooped to pick up his bag.

'Oh, I see. Oh, well, in that case. . .' Kit swallowed against disappointment and faint annoyance as he made his way to the door.

'He's tired out, dear,' Mrs Greenham said, once he'd driven away. 'I could tell that when I was talking to him, and although I'm quite sure he *is* anxious about that accident man I think what he really wants is to get home and be on his own, just for a little while. He's had a shock over this business with Josie, and where there are children involved in any break-up it's more upsetting; it strikes right to the heart.'

'You're right, of course; I'm expecting too much,' Kit said without thinking, causing Mrs Greenham to look at her in surprise.

CHAPTER TEN

Kit moved into Josie's house two weeks later, and a week after that Andrew Gordon moved into his. 'Everyone's gone except us, Daisy,' Mrs Greenham told her little dog one evening. 'Still, we'll have to put up with it.' Philosophical as ever, but feeling a little sad, she went into the garden to water her geraniums and cut a few sweetpeas.

Kit was finding it very different at the Russell Road house without Josie and the boys to keep her company, but it was convenient and comfortable, and she didn't regret the move. What she regretted, or felt rebuffed by, was Richard's attitude. Whenever she saw him at the health centre, or outside in the street, he was always affable, even friendly, but he never sought her out. He seemed to have forgotten, or chosen to forget, what had passed between them; not that very much *had* passed, except that to Kit it had been deeply important, far too important to be written off as pleasant but past and never referred to again.

Of course, he wasn't, she told herself, the kind of man to be able to step blithely and unconcernedly from one girl to another. He might be missing Josie, trying to come to terms with her having decided to back-pedal and remarry Paul. The fact that she, Kit, was living in Josie's house might not help, but that was a small obstacle, surely, and could be easily overcome. No, there was no doubt about it that for the moment, at any rate, he wanted nothing to develop between them, and perhaps he never would.

Sometimes during the long August evenings she took to walking along to Andrew's house at the top of the road to help him with his decorating, and with his garden, which had been neglected and was like a wilderness.

The Brett family were back from Eastbourne and installed in a house in Maida Vale, loaned to them by a friend of Paul's. Kit had been up to see them and found them well and happy—the twins talking of little but going on a big ship to America.

They sailed on the fourth of September, and during the afternoon of that day Kit drove out to Crayton to see Kathleen Revett again. Nearing the house, she had to pull up sharply to avoid a crowd of young people who looked like hippies walking in the road. They scattered when she pipped her horn, making rude signs as she passed, one of the men calling out, 'Nursie, come and massage me, do!'

'They're up at the house on holiday.' Kathleen Revett jerked her head towards Coombe Rise. 'And a rowdy lot they are too. You should hear the noise they make when they come home from the pub at night. Ever so many people have complained, and what sort of state that house must be in I daren't for the life of me think.'

'They may not be staying long,' Kit said sympathetically. Kathleen Revett was inclined to be nervy, and needed all the rest she could get.

'They've been here ten days, so perhaps they'll be going at the end of the week, and it won't be too soon so far as the folk round here are concerned. They have pop music going all night, and although they're two fields off you can still hear it. One night they had the police up there.'

'Perhaps the next lot of holiday people will be really quiet,' Kit said. 'Meanwhile, so far as you're concerned, you're doing well on all fronts.'

'Front being the operative word!' Kathleen managed to laugh. 'I saw Dr Richard at his surgery last week, and he was very pleased with me. He knows you'll be with me when I start labour, and he said I'd be in good hands. Well, what he actually said was, I couldn't be in *better* hands.'

'That was nice of him.' Kit's heart missed a beat, and just for a second the clasps on her case blurred over as she bent to fasten them. 'Now, remember,' she told Kathleen, as they stood at the garden gate, 'remember to get in touch with me when you start having regular pains.'

'I'm unlikely to forget.' Kathleen grimaced, watching Kit get in the car, a little reluctant to see her drive away.

A man and a girl in a hard and fast clinch stood at the side of the road, uninhibitedly necking, oblivious of passers-by. They were probably from the house on the hill. What went on behind its newly painted exterior didn't leave much to the imagination, Kit mused, as she turned down Riverside Lane.

The Libbotses' old bungalow was empty and had a 'FOR SALE' board attached to its stilts. Jill and baby Gemma, Kit knew, had moved down to Portsmouth now. Further along at the donkey sanctuary she caught sight of Rose Garner working alongside a dark-skinned young man who was stripped to the waist. They were filling up the water troughs, while a line of patient donkeys, flicking their tails to keep off the flies, waited to slake their thirst. Baby Tom was there—Kit could see his pram standing in the shade of two big elm trees—and, wanting to see him again, she stopped, and got out, and called Rose's name, waving by the paddock gate.

Rose turned, saw her, said something to her companion, and came racing over the grass. 'Hello. . . Hello, what are you doing here? Come in!' She unhitched the gate.

'I was here in the district, thought I'd stop and see Tom, *and* you, of course.'

'Great!' Rose looked slimmer than when Kit had seen her at the fair. She had a golden-brown tan, and was wearing brief shorts and a button-down-the-front top. They began to walk over to the stables and sheds. 'You can meet Rod, too,' Rose said. 'He's Italian and he goes to a language school in town. He comes here in his spare time. We get along all right.'

'That's nice for you, Rose.'

'And for him too,' she grinned. 'He's learnt a lot from me.' She lifted Tom from his pram, cuddling him briefly before handing him over to Kit—a plump, rubbery baby, with a gummy smile that showed dimples, one on each side of his mouth.

He weighed heavy in Kit's arms. 'He's super, Rose.'

'He's just over three months now.'

'Yes, of course, he must be.' He smelled of hay and of milk.

'I'm still feeding him, so I can't go topless.' Rose flung Kit a wicked look. 'The Miss Cartwrights would have a fit, anyway, and Rod might be put off his stroke.'

'I dare say.' Kit looked over to where the young Italian was stroking the nose of one of the donkeys, while persuading its foal to drink. Rose called him, introducing Kit when he was still yards away. 'This is the nurse who looked after me when Tom was born.'

Rodrigo Manelli rubbed his hand down his jeans before offering it to Kit. 'How do you do?' he said very correctly, making Rose giggle, but he took her merriment in good part, going on to say that he was over in England to get his English exactly right. 'I work in my father's bank in Lugano. To know several languages is of great use as Lugano is a holiday town.'

'Yes, of course.' Kit smiled back into his olive-skinned face, liking its openness and the directness of his gaze. His eyes were sloe-black and thickly lashed; he was about twenty years old.

'I go home at the end of the month.' He was finding it easy to talk to Kit, but he had to break off as the elder Miss Cartwright was calling him from the house. 'Please excuse me,' he said, including Rose in this, then walked off, pulling on a T-shirt as he went.

'He's got lovely manners.' Rose sighed.

'Yes, he certainly has.'

'And when he goes back to Italy Tom and I will be going with him.'

'*Will* you?' Kit's eyes widened.

'Oh, it's all on the level,' Rose laughed. 'I've met his folk. They came over here last month; they offered me a job. I'm to look after their younger children, live as one of the family. They've got a boy of six and a girl of two—born a long time after Rod. I've been wanting something like this for ages.'

'Yes, I remember you saying,' Kit said carefully, 'but what do your parents say?'

'Oh, Mum's creating—you know what she's like—but my dad thinks it's OK. They both met Rod's people, so they know who I'm going to. I've got to think of myself now, make a new life. Tom will love the sunshine and company, and so will I.'

She'll probably fall in love with Rodrigo, if she hasn't already, Kit thought. She watched Rose putting Tom back in his pram, noticing the competent way she handled him, and the soft look in her eyes. 'I wish you every happiness,' she said. 'You deserve it, and I think you're doing the right thing for yourself and Tom.'

'Thanks for what you did for me,' Rose said awkwardly, offering her hand as Rod had done when they said goodbye at the gate.

Two evenings later Kit was driving back to Melbridge after seeing her mother, when she caught sight of Richard and his father crossing over to the Bridge Hotel. A glimpse only was all she got of Richard's head and shoulders, but it was enough to drain her mouth dry, and to cause her heart to turn over in solid lumps, as though it were made of dough. It's nothing less than pathetic to be so affected by a man, she muttered out loud, feeling angry as she turned into Josie's drive.

The phone rang almost as soon as she got into the hall. It was Kathleen Revett's husband, 'Kath's started,' he said; he sounded excited. 'Can you come? I think it's time; she's been having pains regularly since half-past five.'

'How often are they coming?' Kit sighed a little; it was a warm, sticky evening.

'Every ten minutes.'

'All right, I'll be over. I'm starting off now.' Picking up her case again, she went out to the car, rolling down the windows to try to cool it down. What a night to be giving birth—sweated labour indeed.

It was just on eight o'clock when she got to the Revetts' house, and the door was opened before she reached it by Kathleen herself. 'I don't know what you're going to say,' she burst out, 'but the pains are stopping. I haven't had one since Ian rang you. I'm terribly sorry!'

'Oh, don't be; it happens.' Kit stepped into the house. 'False alarms are quite the fashion during the last few weeks. Still now that I'm here I might as well have a look at you, if I may, and stay for a little while, just to make perfectly sure.'

'We'd like that, wouldn't we, Kath?' Ian Revett's face was a good deal more pale and agitated than his wife's. 'Let me get you something—something cold to drink.'

'There's some squash in the fridge,' Kathleen said, and he went out to get it, while Kit took her blood-pressure and listened to her baby's heart.

She had a slight contraction twenty minutes later, and an even slighter one half an hour after that, and then no more. Kit stayed with her until nine-fifteen, when she was completely free of pain and apologetic all over again, standing at the open front doors as she always did, all but filling it with her girth.

Darkness had fallen—the peony sun had set over an hour ago—but the night was still uncomfortably warm, and Kit thought longingly of the tepid shower she would have once she got home. Josie's house had all mod cons, and thank heaven for that.

The light from the Revetts' hall shone her down to the gate, then a figure slanted out of the shadows, and she jumped, and let out a gasp. It was a girl—one of the holiday hippies. Kit could see her bush of hair and skinny outline as she came up close. 'Can you come. . . please. . .quick. . .up there!' She pointed back at Coombe Rise. 'My sister's having a kid, and it's comin'. . . I can see its head!'

It was a cry for help, if ever there was one, and Kit didn't hesitate. 'Get in the car; we'll drive up, be quicker!' She reversed and turned into the lane that led to the house. 'Is this her first child?' she asked.

'Yes, and it shouldn't have come till next week.'

'Where are you from? Who's her doctor?' The car was rocking like a ship at sea, its headlamps swinging searchlight beams over the fields.

'London—Plovers Green; our doctor's name is Stevens.'

'So your sister has been having proper care—has been going to the clinics?'

'One or two, not a lot.'

Kit's heart sank. 'What age. . .how old is she?'

'Twenty, and she wants the kid. Her fella's with her, but he's useless, scared rigid.' The girl's lip curled in the dark. 'She never had no warning, only started having pains two hours ago, then her waters broke, and I see your car. . . I knew you was a nurse.' All this came out in a tumbling rush, punctuated only by the jolting of the car.

Drawing up outside the house, it seemed to Kit that

the garden was full of people—some strolling about, some sprawled on the grass, some standing over a barbecue. Motorbikes were piled up by the fence, and a caravan was parked at the side. Pop music beat out from a transister radio, but not all that loudly, Kit noticed in some relief.

She followed the girl into the house through a line of staring faces. The hall was littered with sleeping-bags, and clothes draped the banisters. There was a smell of curry and stale smoke, while from the bedroom off the landing came the unmistakable sounds of a woman in second-stage labour.

A dark-haired youth with a plait was standing in the doorway. 'Thought you was never coming, Reen!' He looked green and terrified. Kit pushed past him into the room, going straight to the girl on the bed, who looked equally terrified. She was struggling to sit up.

'It's coming. . .it's coming!'

'It's all right, it's all right. I'm here; I'm a nurse. You're in safe hands now!'

'It hurts. . .it hurts. . .it's coming now!' The contraction took hold, mounted and gripped, and at its height Kit was left in no doubt that what was emerging from the girl's straining body was not the head of her child, but its bottom. . . It was going to be a breech birth.

She was dismayed, even alarmed, for although she'd delivered a breech before it had been in hospital with the mother in lithotomy and every medical aid to hand. She took quick stock of the room, which did little to reassure her. Under the mother, whose name she presently ascertained was Jean, were sheets of old newspaper fast getting crumpled up. There was a second bed, and a stout chest of drawers. The floor covered with vinyl, its pattern streaky under a layer of dust. The only good thing was the ceiling light, which was strong and unshaded. At least I'll be able to see what I'm doing, she muttered half to herself. She opened her case, looking over at Reenie, who was holding her sister's hand, 'Are you on the phone here?' A shake of the head answered this. 'In that case someone must go back to the house where you picked me up, and ask the people there to ring for a doctor, because I may need some help. The nearest one is Dr Milton; they must tell him that Midwife Greenham is at Coombe House delivering a breech, and can he come at once.'

'I'll get Ted to go; he's got a bike.' The girl turned to the door.

'And when you've done that bring me two bowls of water—one of hot and one of cold—all the clean towels you can find, a carton box and a liner. Meantime——' she bent over Jean as her sister sped off '—we'll get this vest right off you, and have you standing up, over by this chest here, facing it, gripping its top. That's right, that's exactly right, feet nice and wide apart. That's good, that's really terrific. I'll be behind you here, guiding your baby as you push him out. No, a breech birth doesn't matter—not in the least, not a scrap,' she lied. 'It'll just feel peculiar when his legs drop down—a sort of tickling feeling. That's it. . . they're coming now. . .they're *out*. . . You're doing well!'

He or she was being born facing Kit, who was kneeling on the floor. With each contraction more emerged, till she was able to tell the now shouting mother that she was giving birth to a girl. 'Jean, you're a wonder, you really are; everything's going fine!' Things were moving so fast. . .and furiously. . .and noisily that she hardly noticed Reenie coming in and out, bringing towels, and water and soap. There was no room in her mind for anything but the baby hanging in front of her who, with the next contraction, dropped to umbilicus level. Carefully she freed a loop of cord to prevent it being pulled.

'A towel, please, Reenie,' she hissed, without looking round, but the hand that passed it to her was masculine, a masculine hand that she knew—Richard's hand! Oh, bliss! Oh, joy! He was squatting beside her. There was no time to greet him, though, no time to wonder how he could be here instead of Dr Milton, for more and more of the baby was being born, and now she was able, as the shoulders slipped through, to wrap the towel round the slippery hanging body.

Richard, flinging his jacket off, moved round to the front of the mother, taking her hands from the tallboy chest and putting them round his neck. 'Hang on to me; I'm better than that thing any day of the week!' he told her reassuringly, feeling her hands bite into his flesh as she bore down with the next pain.

Once the child was dangling from the neck down, he and Kit bent the mother over the bed, tilting her pelvis, bringing the baby's nose and mouth peeling into view. Kit sucked these out, listening to Richard encouraging Jean. 'You're nearly done, you're nearly there. . .one more pain. . .one more last effort. . .that's it, that's it. . .good girl!' The head was coming. . .was coming. . . was coming, and, with Richard to assist, Kit was able to deliver it slowly, and prevent it shooting out in an uncontrolled way, which might have caused intracranial haemorrhage.

'You're a brave young woman.' Richard helped Jean lie back on the bed, Kit giving her the baby still attached by its cord, and placing it on her front. After a minute's silence it was yelling lustily. The cord was clamped and cut. Kit wrapped her in the last of the clean towels, and the mother suckled her as though she'd been doing it all her life.

'I wanted a little girl,' she said, almost too spent to speak.

'Well, now you have one. Congratulations, Jean.' Kit smiled down at her. Reenie came in, having heard the baby's cries. A cheer came up from the garden. It was a good moment, a lovely moment—different from the norm, it was true, but lovely for all that—a new baby had been born.

'I don't know what's happened to Ted,' Reenie said, but the mother, engrossed in her baby, and her weariness, didn't seem to care.

'Could you leave us, please, while we finish off?' Richard asked Reenie, a little pointedly; she was smoking a cigarette.

'If you like,' she said, and went off to find Ted, while the remainder of the birthing process—delivering the placenta, inserting a stitch into Jean's fourchette skin, making her comfortable, changing her bed, disposing of 'the bits'—was undertaken by Kit and Richard, working in unison.

At the end of it all, half an hour before midnight, leaving mother and baby asleep, they went downstairs into the odorous kitchen to sluice their hands and arms.

'I was so pleased to see you when you came; I don't

think,' Kit enthused, 'that I've ever been so pleased to see anyone in the whole of my life!' Still drunk on euphoria and relief, it was easy to say these things, so it was like being splashed with cold water when Richard, rolling down his sleeves, and reaching for his jacket, said in a chippy tone of voice,

'Wouldn't it have been better to have sent for me *before* coming up here? Even for a first-rate midwife, which you are, tackling a breech birth without back-up obstetric aid, is just a shade unwise.'

'I had no idea it was going to be a breech until I saw her. All I knew was the girl, Reenie, was terrified out of her wits, shouting that the baby's head was showing! I could hardly delay after that!'

'I see.'

'So how was it *you* came instead of Dr Milton? It was him I expected. I sent one of the boys down to the Revetts' to ask them to phone and get him to help me with a breech birth.'

'I set off as soon as I got Ian Revett's call. He and his wife saw you snatched at their gate—at least, that was how they put it. They rang me even as they saw you driving up here. They had heard the girl say something about a baby, but thought it might be a hoax to get you up here. Mrs Revett was very upset.'

'They're a nervous couple.' Kit warmed to him again, for he'd come, hadn't he? It would have been easier for him to tell Ian Revett to ring Dr Milton and wash his hands of the whole business. She tried the effect of a smile.

He wasn't looking at her; he was putting on his jacket. 'So if you sent for Milton, why hasn't he got here?' he asked in the same chippy tone.

'I've no idea.' Her chin went up. Did he think she was telling lies?

'Ted couldn't get no reply from that house; they wouldn't answer the door.' Reenie sauntered in from the garden and leaned against the sink. 'He even banged on a window and called through the letter-box, but they told him to clear off or they'd get the police, so he gave up, and went down to the pub.'

'So much for your messenger,' Richard said softly.

'Where is Ted now?' Kit felt angry, tired and hot, and at odds with the lot of them.

'Upstairs with Jean. He's not a bad bloke; he minds about her, and he's ever so pleased about the baby, but he just gets scared.' Having delivered her piece, Reenie went back to the crowd in the garden. If the nurse and that la-di-da doctor were going to have a row, let them bloody get on with it; it was nothing to do with her.

But it wasn't a row—nothing like a row—yet it had that feel about it. Kit was certain that Richard was burning to say far more than he was. He wanted to carp, and be critical. She could see it in his face, sense it in his hard-eyed manner, and, exhausted though she was, she longed to provoke him, to make him say it, to force it out of him.

'Are you staying?' he asked, when she made no move to follow him out of the house.

'For a time, yes. I've not done yet; I need to make up my notes. My supervisor will have to know about the birth, and my part in it. It's possible—being the end of the week tomorrow—that this crowd will be moving out, so the midwives at the London end will need to be notified.'

'I'll contact the mother's GP, of course.'

'Yes, I rather thought you would. I'll leave his details at the health centre tomorrow.'

'Thank you very much.'

There was a moment when they measured glances, standing there on the step, with the garden full of revellers, with the music turned up full pitch, with the moon reclining on its back high above the trees.

'Goodnight, and thank you for coming.' Kit was determined to be polite, and perhaps he was too, for he took the trouble to tell her that she'd done a splendid job, but it didn't sound in the least like praise—not in the way he said it. It sounded more like a grudging appeasement; it sounded like a sop.

CHAPTER ELEVEN

As from Tuesday of the following week Kit was asked to take a student midwife under her wing. Anna Slade—from the County Hospital—was just starting her community experience. She was a likeable girl, very anxious to learn, and Kit took to her at once. It was pleasant, she found, to have someone in the car with her when she went out on visits. Anna's manner with the mothers and their babies and the way she handled the latter impressed Kit, and augured well for the future, she felt.

After the clinic on Wednesday, at which Anna helped, Kit made a special point of telling her about Kathleen Revett, due to give birth in two weeks' time. 'She's booked for a domino delivery, so with luck you'll be on hand to help me with the first part of her labour at home.' She gave Anna her notes to read, then mentioned Eve Taylor. 'She'll be the icing on the cake so far as you're concerned, Anna, for she's having a home birth. She's due in ten days, but it could be sooner; it'll be her fourth child. She's Austrian-born, married to a milkman. They've got a houseful of pets, including a parrot, would you believe?'

'Sounds fun,' Anna laughed. 'Who's her GP?'

'Dr Richard Anstey.' Kit managed to bring out his name without a tremor. 'But he won't be present at the birth unless there are complications, which I don't anticipate. . .not like last Friday, when I was pitchforked into delivering a breech at a minute's notice, with no knowledge of the mother's history.' She told Anna about the birth at Coombe Rise, how she'd had to send for assistance, and how Richard had come. She didn't bother to explain about Ted's useless efforts.

'Weren't you frightened?'

'Terrified.'

'Still, you coped.'

'Yes, with help, I did.'

'And they were all right—the mother and baby?'

'Absolutely fine. They went back home the very next day, but the health visitor and I were able to check them over before they set off. They travelled in a caravanette—like a van with let-down bunks. We alerted the community team at the Plovers Green end, so they would know they needed visiting for the next week or two. We even got together some handed-down clothes for the baby. Neither Megan nor I could bear the thought of her arriving at her home for the very first time rolled up in an old piece of vest!'

'Heavens, what an experience!'

'Yes, you can say that again.'

'You mentioned Dr Anstey; he's nice, isn't he?' Anna moved the weighing machine back against the wall, turning to Kit, who was through in the ante-room, standing at the sink.

'Oh, very nice, yes.' Her voice sounded muffled.

'I met him when I was doing my initial period at the hospital. He came up and gave a lecture one night, and there was a discussion afterwards. Everyone raved about him.'

'I can imagine that they would.' Kit sterilised the last

of the specimen jars, keeping her back towards Anna till she'd got her face under control.

She hadn't seen Richard since Friday night, up at Coombe Rise, when he'd nit-picked about how she'd acted in the way of summoning aid. He had seemed to want to fault-find; he had seemed hell-bent on driving an impenetrable wedge between them, to prevent her drawing close. They had been close during that difficult birth, during that marvellous moment when a perfect child had emerged and been given to its mother. They had been close, too, during the third stage, and cleaning up afterwards. But afterwards, no. . . Downstairs, no. Downstairs in that smelly kitchen he had deliberately pricked her balloon of happiness and then taken himself off home.

There are times when I don't even like him, much less love him, she thought, saying goodnight to Anna, and going out to the car.

He was in the public library on Thursday, just after five o'clock. She had gone there to return some books for Andrew. They often did small errands for one another, as they lived so close. She spotted Richard as she stood at the counter waiting to hand the books in. He was over in the biography section, and the sight of his long, lean back, the set of his head and the movement of his shoulders as he pulled out a book riveted all her attention, made her lose her place in the queue, made her—as though drawn by a cord—go over and speak to him.

'Hello, Richard.' Her voice came out more like a raven's croak. As for him, he tensed and stood stock-still, before he turned slowly round.

'Why, Kit, hello.' He smiled; so did she. Then he

looked at the small pyramid of books wedged against her hip. 'You're on the same game as me!'

'Well, no, not really.' She hitched them up. 'These are Andrew's books. I'm returning them for him. He's busy at the moment, getting ready for the start of term.'

'Ah, yes, the autumn term. Time goes very quickly.'

'It does; I can hardly believe I've been living in. . . Russell Road nearly six weeks.' In the nick of time she stopped herself from saying, 'In Josie's house'. It could be a thin-ice subject, she felt, and when he made a movement back to the shelves she turned away, only to hear him ask,

'Have you heard from Josie yet? How are they all getting on?'

'I went up to see them when they were in London.' She retraced her steps. 'They were fine. Josie was looking much more. . .robust. Actually they should be in America by now; they sailed last week.'

'The sea trip will put the finishing touch to Jo's convalescence,' he said.

'As well as delighting the twins; you know what they are about boats.'

'I do.' He slid the book he was holding back on the shelf. He took out another, but didn't open it. 'I miss them very much.'

'Oh, so do I,' she assured him quickly. 'It doesn't seem the same without them.' And she meant what she said, for sometimes the house took on a haunted quality when she fancied she could hear the thud of little boys' feet on the stairs, hear their voices, faint and far off, in the bedroom opposite hers. Still, she could hardly tell him that, could she? What she eventually said was that Josie had given her some snaps of the boys taken at the address they had lived at in London. 'They're really very good indeed. Would you like to see them?' And please, she prayed, let him say yes. Let him want to see them, and ask me out, ask me to bring them, make it a proper date.

'I'd love to see them.' His answer was prompt, and hope rose in Kit, only to be stifled at birth by his turning back to the shelves, and saying over his shoulder, 'Why not drop them in at the health centre some time? I'll see that you get them back.'

'Good idea, I'll do that,' she managed to reply. She managed to get to the counter too, and hand in the books, and get the little cardboard tickets, and stumble out into the street.

It was another turn-off. He didn't want her company; he was bent on showing her that. She was foolish and lacking in proper pride to keep putting herself on the line. At first she had thought he was still hankering after Jo, but now she wasn't so sure. What she *was* sure of was that what he'd once felt for her was no longer there. He neither wanted nor needed her now. And the sooner I face up to that, the better, she thought, with a touch of bravado, pushing against the pain of rejection as she walked through the crowded streets.

Work would help; work always did. Work was the panacea. She was glad she was extra busy next day, when her thoughts and feelings had to be trained on the mothers who needed her expertise. And then shortly after she got home she received a call from the midwives' base to say that Eve Taylor had gone into labour. Good, she thought, good for Eve. And, quickly checking over the contents of her obstetric bag, she went out to get the car.

She picked up her student—Anna Slade—*en route*, and off they set in the hot dark evening that seemed to be threatening a storm. 'I'm so thrilled to be in on a home birth,' enthused Anna. 'It's so different in hospital.'

'As chalk from cheese.' Kit dipped her lights as they turned into the High Street. 'But at one time, long before your or my time, having babies at home was the norm. Now it's fairly unusual, which is a pity in some ways.'

Anna had met Eve Taylor on Tuesday, and said how much she liked her. 'She's quite a character.'

'Yes, Eve's a dear, takes everything in her stride. It's a shame it's such a humid night—not for us, but for her sake, I mean.' And actually, Kit thought, it wasn't unlike last Friday night, when she, with Richard's help, had delivered the baby up at Coombe Rise. Was it really only a week ago? It seemed more like years.

When they reached the house the children were still up, and so were the animals. One of the little girls came to the door, looked frightened and awed. Eve and her husband, and the small boy, James, were through in the sitting-room, looked down on by the baleful parrot side-stepping on his perch. Eve, fully dressed, was prowling round the room, and just as Kit and Anna entered she leaned against the sideboard, doing her best not to groan.

As the contraction passed Kit persuaded her to transfer upstairs. 'You can walk about up there just the same, if you like, but you'll be quieter, and we can get you undressed and the children into bed.'

'Yes, I go while the going iss good,' Eve agreed, kissing each of the children, and managing the flight of stairs on all fours, with Kit and Anna and an anxious Bill Taylor bringing up the rear.

The 'labour' bedroom was scrupulously clean; Eve had followed all Kit's advice. There were two cleared table surfaces, the bed was covered with polythene, and there were bowls and jugs, buckets and basins, towels, a nailbrush and soap; there were even two comfortable chairs for the midwives-in-waiting. 'You're a gem, Eve.' Anna helped her undress and put on a short cotton nightie. Kit took her temperature, pulse and blood-pressure, palpated her abdomen, and examined her internally, donning sterile gloves.

'Everything's spot-on,' she declared. 'The baby's head is engaged, and you're dilating slowly but surely. Now, what I'd like you to do is go along to the bathroom with Bill and try to spend a penny. It'll be midnight, at earliest, before she's in second stage,' she remarked to Anna, once Eve was out of the room, 'so we might as well get those children to bed, and make sure they've had something to eat.'

'I'll do that,' Anna offered, just as a gust of wind blew in through the open sash window, overturning a jug.

'It's blowing up for a storm.' Kit shut the window to all but a tiny crack. Anna went down to see to the children. Eve and Bill came back from the bathroom.

'She's had another pain.' Bill looked racked.

'Which make one pain less,' Eve managed to say, dropping down on all fours as another contraction took hold.

The night wore on. The wind came in flurries—one minute there and then gone. . .on and off. . .on and off—as though the very heavens were puffing and blowing, pushing and groaning, trying to give birth to a storm.

It was hot in the little bedroom, airless and uncomfortable. Kit's and Anna's dresses were sticking to them, as they encouraged and soothed a sweating Eve, who was fast approaching the end of first stage labour. 'Leave the door ajar when you go down; we'll get in as much air as we can,' Kit said to Anna, who was going downstairs to make them all drinks. She brought up a glucose one for Eve, squash for herself and Kit, and Alka-Seltzer for Bill Taylor, who complained of feeling sick. The house was a tall thin one, with a second storey. The children's bedrooms were up there, so even with the door open they were fairly unlikely to hear what was going on. Bill had plans to join the children. He didn't feel able to take much more of this hassle. . . He'd be better upstairs with the kids.

He made a move when he saw the equipment being set out for the birth. 'He has not the stomach for it; he was the same in hospital!' Eve gasped and struggled to sit up. 'It is coming. . .it is coming *now*!' And it was, but so was the storm. As the baby's head crowned, the lightning flashed, followed by a clap of thunder so loud that it drowned Eve's grunts and shouts, drowned the midwives' voices, and brought the dog flying up from the downstairs regions to shelter under the bed, followed by a fear-crazed cat and kittens, all rushing to the same safe harbour. 'All we need now is the parrot to complete the menagerie!' Kit wasn't best pleased, but told Anna to leave them where they were. 'We haven't got time to bother with. . . Quick, pass me that inco pad. . . It's all right, Eve, love. You're doing fine; you're being so good!'

With the next contraction the baby's face appeared and, with some help from Kit, his chin. The storm raged overhead. 'Perhaps it is the end of the world,' gasped Eve, who probably thought it was. She was still having contractions and was pushing strongly with each one, but nothing was happening; the child wasn't coming any further out. As none of his neck could be seen Kit couldn't feel for the cord.

'The shoulders are wide and they're wedged,' she said aside to Anna. 'We've got to get them rotating; we must move her.' She bent to talk to Eve. 'You're going to have to do some rock and rolling, Eve, to help get baby born. Anna and I will help you roll over. . . no, you can keep on the bed. . .gently does it. . . Now up on your knees. . .on all fours—that's it! Lean over to me. . .now to Anna. . .now back to me. . .and here he comes, and here he comes! A lovely little boy!'

Eve slumped back and they gave her the child, who very soon started to cry. Eve did too. She wept all over him, holding him to her breast. 'I cry tears of joy,' she said, as Anna wiped them away, 'and thank you for all you did for me, and for getting him born.'

There was more to do yet—there was still the third stage—but it was soon over and done. Eve was made comfortable and the baby washed and weighed. 'Ten pounds, what a whopper! I hope he'll fit these clothes,' Kit said, dressing him, and handing him back to his mother. Anna went upstairs to tell Bill, and he came down with the three children. The dog and the cats came from under the bed, as the thunder and lightning had ceased. The whole family gathered round the bed to welcome the new arrival, and for a few minutes Kit and Anna tactfully left the room.

By the time they had cleared everything away, and gone back upstairs to turn the birthing bed into a sleeping one with a duvet and sheet, it was very nearly five a.m. and they were glad to fall in with Bill Taylor's request and stay until breakfast-time.

'I like to stay on for about an hour after a home birth, in any case,' Kit said to Anna as, downstairs in the sitting-room, they made themselves comfortable in deep easy-chairs.

'It was a big baby, and Eve didn't need stitches, all due to you,' Anna said.

'You helped; that made an enormous difference.'

'I was thrilled to be in on it.' Anna undid her belt and kicked off her shoes. Neither girl could sleep, but at least they could relax in the knowledge that everything had gone well.

Upstairs in the big double bed, Bill and Eve Taylor lay with their arms about one another, while in the frilled bassinet, with its blue ribbons and blue blanket, their baby son slept away the trauma of getting himself born.

The three other children were back in their beds, the tall thin house was safe and snug, warm and dry, and full of beautiful feelings. Outside the rain slammed down, and it was only just easing when at eight-thirty, with mother and baby bathed and made comfortable, Kit and Anna prepared to leave the house. Mrs Ida Taylor, Bill's mother, had arrived to take charge.

'Terrible storm, wasn't it?' she said. 'Two trees in the park were struck by lightning, and parts of Crayton had no electricity for a time. Someone told me a house was struck, but I don't know how true that is.'

Thank heavens we were all right for electricity, Kit

thought as she drove, splurging through lakes of water at times, towards the hospital. There, at the midwives' base, they signed off duty, made sure that Eve would be visited by one of the team at lunchtime, and asked that Richard, who was Eve's GP, should be informed of the birth.

It occurred to Kit that she could call at the health centre and tell Richard herself, but she decided against this, for, it being a Saturday, he might not be there, and in any case it wasn't necessary, nor part of her job. She was only looking for an excuse to see him, thereby risking another of those awful polite conversations, which she didn't feel she could stand.

Another midwife, setting off on her visits, offered to run Anna home, and Kit was just about to get in her car and drive home to Grantford, where she was spending the weekend with her mother, when a young nurse, whom she knew by sight, called to her from the entrance to A and E.

'Excuse me.' She ran towards Kit, holding on to her cap. 'I think you're a friend of a patient who was admitted last night. You *are* Kit Greenham?'

'Yes, I am.' Kit stared back into the girl's spotty face. 'Who. . .is the patient?' Her words came in jerks.

'A Mr Andrew Gordon; he's been asking for you. His house was damaged last night. The chimney was struck by lightning and came through the roof. He's not badly hurt,' she added quickly, seeing Kit's face go white.

Kit moved. She felt herself doing so, felt the nurse take her arm. 'I should have waited until you were sitting down; I've given you a shock.'

'I'm all right. I want to see him. Is he in the emergency ward?'

'No, Observation, but I don't think. . .'

Kit set off for Casualty, got through the doors, crossed the big waiting hall, swerved round the desk and walked through the aisle between the cubicles and out to the bay with its swing-doors marked: 'Observation and Emergency Wards'.

The staff nurse in charge was getting ready for the doctors' round. She, too, knew Kit by sight. 'You can pop in for five minutes,' she said, taking a look through the viewing window to make sure the young Scotsman was awake.

Andrew's left arm was in a sling, his forehead and ear were bandaged, and there were cuts and grazes on his other arm. He looked shocked and vulnerable, leaning against a bank of pillows, wearing a hospital gown. He saw Kit coming. 'You heard, then?' He watched her pull up a chair.

'Just now. Oh, Andrew, what an awful thing to happen, but thank goodness you were living downstairs!' She took his less damaged hand, careful of the bruises that were already beginning to show.

'Even so, I had a lucky escape. If I'd been in the kitchen, where the chimney plunged through, I wouldn't be here now. I was in bed, and that was bad enough. Part of the inside wall collapsed and fell in on me. . .or, at least, so I've been told.'

'Do they say how you are. . .what your injuries are?' His hand felt very cold.

'Just that there are no bones broken. I was X-rayed last night. I expect the doctors will see me this morning, but I think it's mostly cuts. I was covered in soot when I came in, which didn't help very much.'

It wasn't helping him to talk, either. Kit could see that plainly enough, but he was bent on telling her all about it, so she let him go on for a bit. 'The Ramshaws opposite hauled me out and called the ambulance. Oh, Kit, when I think. . .all our decorating, all our hard work gone to waste!'

'That doesn't matter; it can be put right, Andrew. You might have been killed! If you'd been living upstairs and not down, it doesn't bear thinking about.'

'I can put in a claim. I'm well insured; I believe in insurance. Kit—' he leaned forward, dislodging a pillow, which she quickly put back into place '—on your way home, could you go in—into the house, I mean? I've got the keys; they're in my locker. I need some pyjamas, and some day clothes too, for when they let me out.'

'Why, yes, of course. . .'

'And could you make sure there's a tarpaulin on the roof? The Ramshaws said they'd get a builder on to it, but could you make sure?'

'I will, and I'll have a proper look round.' Kit put the keys into her bag.

'I knew you'd help me. . . It's a weight off my mind. Thanks for coming in.'

'But now I must turn her out.' Staff Nurse appeared at the foot of the bed. Kit got up at once, kissed Andrew's cheek, and, telling him that all he had to do was get well, she quietly left the ward.

Russell Road was a through road, and she drove in past Josie's house, thankful to see that all was well there, but a very different sight met her eyes when she got to the top of the road. There was a builders' lorry outside Andrew's house; a tarpaulin hung over the roof. Where the upstairs bay window had been was a great gaping hole with tatters of black curtains flying out in the wind. Round at the back—and it was all she could do to make herself walk round there—the builders were boarding up windows and doors, crunching on top of broken glass, coughing through billows of soot.

'If you want to go in, miss,' the elder builder said, when she explained why she had come, 'you'll have to use the front door. And mind how you go—there's a wall inside that might fall down on you.'

Kit went in, gingerly in, then stood aghast, scarcely recognising the hall and stairs, which were carpeted in soot. The sitting-room was reasonably clean, but Andrew's bedroom across the hall and next door to the kitchen had rubble and glass all over the bed, and still more soot; it seemed to hang in clouds. Through the hole in the wall she could see the chimney sitting in the kitchen, broken into chunks, half embedded in the floorboards. Never had she realised that chimney stacks were as big as that, or could demolish a room and its contents, as this one had done. There was nothing in the kitchen that Kit could recognise. Something drew her glance upwards through the kitchen ceiling, or what was left of it, through the bedroom ceiling which was no longer there, up into the loft, to the roof itself with its smashed rafters, to the underside of the blue tarpaulin, which was keeping out the rain.

It was upsetting in a way she couldn't explain. She felt shaky and sick at heart as she groped about in Andrew's bedroom, finding suitable clothes, and night things too, and a bag to put them in.

She was glad to leave, thankful to leave. She would have to return, of course—she would have to come back to see to things properly—but first she must get some sleep. She couldn't concentrate without any sleep; she might even die on her feet. She had been on the go for twenty-four hours; she must get some sleep or go mad. And she needed company, so Kit decided to go to her mother's.

The mile-long journey home to Grantford through the cool, September morning seemed to go on forever. The rain was easing off. By the time she half fell out of the car in the driveway of Ford House, a thin sunlight was gilding the gravel, silvering the soaking wet lawn.

Mrs Greenham, on hearing what had happened, *and* that Kit had been up all night, sent her upstairs to shower. 'You're as black as a sweep, my child!'

'Well, I know that, don't I. . .? I've been walking around over my ankles in soot!'

'After you've cleaned up, get straight into bed, and I'll bring you some breakfast. Yes, I know it's after ten, but I don't suppose you've had anything, and if you're going to sleep for the next five hours you'll need something to sustain you.'

'Sounds as though I'm hibernating.'

'And while you're in bed I'm going to Melbridge to make sure those builders have left the house quite safe. Andrew won't want squatters, or looters; that's the last thing he needs. Afterwards I'm going into the town to buy him one or two things. I'll have my lunch at the Creamery, then, as soon as it's two o'clock, I'll go to the hospital to visit him, and tell him that once he's discharged he can come back here, live here again until his house is fixed.'

What it is to have a practical mother, Kit thought as she stood under the pelting shower, washing her hair as well, letting the soot and the tensions of the day. . .and the night. . .flow down the drain.

'You don't mind being left until teatime, do you dear?' Mrs Greenham enquired when she brought up Kit's breakfast toast.

'Of course not. Why should I? I'll be asleep; I won't even know. And if the telephone rings it won't be for me, for I'm not on call. I'm not anything. . .' Kit stretched luxuriously '. . .except myself, plain Kit Greenham, until Monday morning at eight. All the same, Mummy, don't go wearing yourself out. You know what you're like when you've got the bit between your teeth, and are bent on doing good works.'

'I must make sure Andrew is all right, dear.' Mrs Greenham picked up the tray. 'I owe it to his mother. I probably ought to put a call through to Edinburgh and let her know.' She went downstairs with solid plops, calling to Daisy, who she knew liked to lie at the foot of her daughter's bed.

Kit slept dreamlessly; the hours slipped by. Shortly after two she heard the telephone ringing down in the hall, but, true to her resolve, she didn't answer it, just slid back into sleep. Daisy's barking woke her next, and, stretching out her arm for her watch on the bedside table, she saw it was three o'clock. She felt refreshed; it was time she got up. Getting dressed in one of the printed cotton frocks she always kept at home, she cleaned her teeth, brushed her hair, and drew the curtains back from the window, not really seeing anything in detail, just lazily taking in the familiar stretch of lawn and flowerbeds striped with the afternoon sun.

Then she saw something. . .saw *someone* standing in the orchard, looking straight towards the house, and she gave a little cry. It was Richard. . .*Richard*! But why had he come, what was he doing here, and why was he standing out in the garden? Something must be wrong.

He had seen her draw the curtains back; he was coming towards the house. She ran downstairs, out of the kitchen door, and up the garden to meet him. He was grave-faced, then half smiling. It was she who spoke first. 'How long have you been here? Is there anything wrong? Why didn't you come to the door?'

'I knew your mother was out—I caught a glimpse of her in the town. I guessed you were sleeping. I heard at the hospital that you'd been up all night.'

'Yes, delivering Mrs Taylor's baby—a ten pound baby boy. She was being checked at lunchtime by one of the team. She *is* all right, isn't she?'

'I'm quite sure she is.' He looked down at her. 'Kit, this is a social call. I felt I had to come after seeing what the lightning did to Gordon's house. I went by on my way home at lunchtime, and got the shock of my life.'

'Yes, so did I. It's awful, isn't it? You should see the inside. But Andrew's not badly hurt, thank goodness. I went in to see him when I was told what had happened, and he asked me to look round.'

'I went in shortly before two, but it was the ward's quiet time. He was asleep, so I didn't disturb him.'

'That was nice of you, but I suppose you were at the hospital anyway.'

'As a matter of fact, no, I wasn't.' He put her straight on that. 'It wasn't until I saw the house that I turned the car and drove there double-quick, fully expecting to see both you and Gordon in A and E.'

'*Both*?' Kit ejaculated.

'Why, yes, because until I got to the hospital I didn't know you'd been out all night. I assumed you'd been there. . .in the house. . .and the thought turned me cold!'

'Look. . . Richard. . .just a minute.' She stopped him walking on. 'Andrew and I aren't lovers. I'm not in the habit of being with him at three in the morning, which was when the chimney was struck.'

'But you live with him!' He made that a statement.

'I assure you I don't. I've been going there, helping him decorate, working in the garden, but I don't live there. I never have. I'm living in Josie's house.'

'*Josie's house*?' He looked electrified.

'I thought you knew.'

'I had no idea!'

'But what made you think I was living with Andrew?'

'Your mother told me so.'

'She couldn't have.' It was Kit's turn to stare. 'She couldn't have, not possibly, Richard; you must have misunderstood.'

He shook his head as though even now he didn't quite believe what he'd heard. 'It was the night I came to see the twins, to say goodbye to them. We were talking in the hall—Mrs Greenham and I. You had gone upstairs. She said she was losing you and Andrew, as well as the twins, but that she mustn't be selfish, because Russell Road was so convenient for you both.'

'Oh, dear, yes.' Kit bit her lip. 'I can see how it happened.'

'I knew Gordon had asked you to share with him; I

thought he'd pulled it off. I also thought that in such close quarters you wouldn't be "just friends" for long.'

'And you didn't approve?' Her eyebrows went up. 'Is that why you've been so anxious to distance me during these last few weeks? I *wondered* why it was!'

'Don't mock; it's not funny. And it's not a case of approval, as you well know!' His words were admonitory, but the look on his face made her catch her breath.

'Let's sit down,' she said quickly. They had reached the patio. 'I'll go and make some tea.'

'No, don't. Leave it. There's something I want to say to you, Kit. . .something I want to explain.' He took her hand as they sat down. The chairs were wet, but neither noticed; all their attention was on one another. Richard felt nervous; there was so much at stake. 'I've been in love with you since that night we put the twins to bed,' he began, 'the night we thought Josie had been to see her parents in town. Afterwards I found out, quite by chance, that it was Paul Brett she'd seen. She's probably told you about it, so I'm not telling tales out of school!'

'Yes, she told me.' Kit's voice was a thread.

'I didn't like being lied to. I began to doubt her word on other issues, probably unfairly. In short, I became suspicious and critical which didn't help things along. Then she got ill, and I was devastated. . .' His fingers tightened round Kit's. 'I used to sit by her bed and think. Of course I love her, and once we're married everything will be all right. She needs taking care of; I'll do that. They were almost vows of a sort. I managed to convince myself that what I was feeling for you was a strong dose of sexual attraction, and nothing, nothing more.

'But I knew it was more than that on the day of the fair, when I ran you back here to change your dress. I didn't dare touch you; I hardly dared look at you in case you saw how I felt. I knew I loved you, but I also knew I could never let Josie down.

'That trip to the zoo was going to be the last outing I'd have with you. I was going to behave impeccably; not by a single look or word or gesture would I step out of line. But we kissed, didn't we? And the skies fell, or so it seemed to me. I couldn't be sure what you felt about me. What I did know was that I'd be doing Jo no favour by marrying her when I wanted you. Yet the thought of breaking with her appalled me. She still wasn't strong, never *would* be quite as strong as she had been, and then there were the boys; they trusted me, relied on me in all sorts of ways. I knew I couldn't live with my conscience if I walked out on them all.'

'I knew that,' Kit broke in. 'Jo was, *is* my friend. I would never have come between you; I'd have gone right away.'

Richard shook his head. He wanted no interruptions; he had *got* to get to the end. 'I was racked with indecision for the rest of our time at the zoo, then we had that fright in the Underground, and when I learned that Brett had been seeing Jo in hospital I began to wonder what was going on, so made up my mind to find out. I went in to see her, and the rest you know. It was she who brought the axe down, telling me she was going to marry Brett.'

He had her other hand now; their knees were touching.

'Is that what you wanted to hear?' Kit asked, still feeling slightly unreal.

'Yes, of course it was, but, human nature being what it is, I felt as though I'd had a knock, but that was male pride, I suppose. I felt justly angry, I felt relieved, then absolutely convinced that it was exactly what was meant to happen, right from the very first.'

'They'll be happy, I'm sure,' Kit said quietly.

'And what about us?'

She met his eyes, then looked down at his hands, tightly clasping hers. 'There's just one thing I don't understand, something that doesn't add up. You've been practically avoiding me these past few weeks because you thought Andrew and I were a couple. And you were still under that impression when you came here this afternoon, yet it didn't *stop* you coming. So what changed your attitude?'

'That damaged house changed it. . .it changed *me*. . . I was shaken to my roots. So, OK, I soon learned you'd been out all night and were nowhere near at the time, but I still had to come; nothing else would do. I had to see for myself that you were safe, that you were all right. I loved you, no matter what!'

'That's a nice thing to say.'

'Nice be damned!' Starting to his feet, he drew her up and out of the chair, and held her close to him, warmly close, enfoldingly close. She sighed and put her arms round his neck and drew his head down to hers. His hair was smooth-rough under her fingers; his cheek was hard against hers.

'I love you,' she said. 'I've loved you dearly since that evening you spoke about, but I didn't know what to do about it, so I went back home to live. You were engaged to Jo. I had to get over you, but I never ever succeeded. I kept losing ground, and it was terrible. Josie was my friend.'

'Dear love, I know, I understand.' He turned her face round to his, closing her eyes with little kisses, touching the tip of her nose, tracing her mouth and then kissing it, drawing her closer still. 'Will you marry me? Will you be my wife? Will you come and live in my house?'

'Yes, I will, to all three questions.' The look in her eyes—tender and teasing, and shining with love for him—made him catch his breath.

'You dwell in my heart,' he told her simply, bringing his mouth to hers in a kiss that set the seal on their love, and time stood still in the way it had done for lovers since the world began.

Mills & Boon